The Key to Popularity

Anna listened to their stories. She looked around at her friends isolated at the small table in the middle of the bustling cafeteria. In their junior high, where they had known almost everyone in their class, the four of them were the center of attention at lunchtime. Here they didn't know two-thirds of the kids, and their former classmates were busy simply trying to recover from the morning and find niches for themselves in the strange environment.

Suddenly, Peggy's words came back to Anna. *The key to popularity.* Anna was holding it in her lap. She peeked down and could see the black-and-white blotches looking back at her. They were practically calling to her.

Other books by
ANN M. MARTIN
you may enjoy:

Just a Summer Romance

Missing Since Monday

With You and Without You

point

SLAM BOOK

Ann M. Martin

SCHOLASTIC INC.
New York Toronto London Auckland Sydney

ISBN 0-590-41838-6

12 11 10 9 8 7 6 5 4 3   9/8 0 1 2 3 4/9

Printed in the U.S.A.   01

First Scholastic printing, August 1989

For JANE, *my sister*

SLAM
BOOK

Chapter One

Anna Wallace often thought—later, after it was all over
—that if she'd known the chain of events the slam book
was going to set in motion, she'd never have gone to the
family picnic. But on that Labor Day weekend, during
those last precious days of summer vacation before she
entered Calvin High School, Anna hadn't even known
what a slam book was.

So she'd gone to the picnic. And that was how it had
all started.

Anna and her parents had driven from Calvin, Penn-
sylvania, to Clearwater, the next town over, for the an-
nual gathering of the Wallace clan. Anna was proud of
her big family—all the aunts and uncles and cousins and
greats and great-greats—but sometimes they could become overwhelming.

It was during the long gap between the serving of lunch and the serving of dessert that Anna decided she'd had enough. She wandered away from a knot of relatives and caught sight of Bucky, her collie, sitting next to the food table, greedily eyeing a platter of cold cuts that had become greasy in the heat.

"You want something?" Anna whispered to him. She knew she wasn't supposed to feed him cold cuts, but he looked so pathetic.

Anna swiped a piece of baloney, rolled it up, held it above Bucky's head, and allowed him to jump for it. Bucky swallowed his prize in an instant.

"How could you even taste that?" Anna asked him at the same time that a voice behind her said, "I saw that!"

Anna whirled around and faced her sister, Hilary. Anna giggled. "You always catch me!"

"You're always doing something to be caught *at*," Hilary replied good-naturedly. She smoothed Anna's hair back from her forehead.

Seth, Hilary's little boy, ran to Anna and wrapped his arms around her legs. "Aunt Annie?" he said.

Anna hoisted him onto her hip. "What, Sethie?"

"Ice cur-ream?" he pronounced carefully.

"Sorry, kiddo," said Hilary, taking him from Anna. "There's no ice cream yet. Besides you've had enough junk today to last you until World War Three."

"Hilary!" exclaimed Anna. "Talk to him so he can understand you. Little kids don't like to be left out of things."

Hilary looked searchingly at her sister. "What are you

saying, toots? Do you feel left out?"

"No. . . . Well, sometimes."

"Gosh. I thought you had it so easy, being the little caboose in our family. You've been practically like an only child since I got married."

"I hate that term—caboose. I'm the youngest kid, that's all. And I don't think I was entirely unexpected, was I?" Anna had asked her parents this question an uncountable number of times, but she wasn't sure she had ever gotten a straight answer.

"Even if you were, it doesn't mean you were unwanted," said Hilary.

Anna glanced around at her relatives. The adults had taken all the food into her aunt Meg and uncle Ray's house. Paper plates and cups and napkins were being whisked into garbage bags. The back door opened, and her aunt emerged with a tray of desserts. Dessert was her specialty.

"I know I wasn't unwanted. . . ." Anna regarded Hilary thoughtfully. Hilary was twenty-three—nine years older than she was. She'd been married for three years. She and her husband, Tom, were expecting another baby in January.

"Anna! Hey, Anna! I've got something to show you!" It was Peggy, Anna's cousin, Aunt Meg and Uncle Ray's daughter. "Get your dessert and let's go up to my room."

Hilary put Seth down and gave Anna a quick hug. "Go on with Peggy," she said. "And if I ever call you our little caboose again, remember that it's a term of affection and that I can't help myself."

"And furthermore," replied Anna, "that it makes you the freight car of the family."

"Very funny," said Hilary, smiling. She patted her bulging stomach.

Peggy took Anna's elbow. "God, what a spread," she exclaimed, guiding her cousin down the length of the newly laden food table, which Bucky was contemplating with a doggie expression that was a mixture of longing and greed. The girls looked at pies, brownies, cookies, ice cream, watermelon slices, blueberry cobbler, and cheesecake. "I don't think there's enough dessert here," said Peggy. "Do you? Maybe I should run out and buy another vat of ice cream."

"Just to be on the safe side," agreed Anna, giggling. Peggy was her favorite cousin. Anna had seventeen cousins, not counting the children of her oldest cousins, who were actually her first cousins once removed. Anna and Peggy were the youngest, so they had a lot in common.

"Seriously, do you want any dessert before we go to my room?" Peggy asked Anna.

"I want everything," Anna replied honestly, "but I'll settle for vanilla ice cream."

"Anna, that is so *bor*ing."

"It's always been my favorite," Anna said defensively. She helped herself to ice cream, while Peggy cut a wedge of cheesecake.

"Hey, Anna, grab your dish and let's go," Peggy said suddenly, under her breath. "Aunt Sophie's heading over here."

Anna didn't hesitate. She dashed after Peggy, who was heading for the back door of her house. Sophie was the oldest of the aunts and smelled of cough medicine and lavender toilet water—a lousy combination on a hot day. Also, she was sprouting whiskers on her chin and had picked up on every bad old-lady habit Anna could think of. She tucked Kleenex under the sleeves of her dress, wore baggy stockings, and dyed her hair so that it was tinged with blue. Occasionally, she put on a hair net.

Anna had never told anyone, but what she disliked most about Sophie was that when her aunt was young she looked just like Anna. (Anna had compared photographs.) So Anna was afraid she would grow up to become another Sophie—a scary thought, when what she wanted to be was popular.

Anna and Peggy clattered up the stairs to Peggy's room and flopped on her bed with their desserts. Peggy ate lying on her stomach.

"How can you do that?" asked Anna. "I've never understood how anyone can eat in a prone position."

"It aids digestion," replied Peggy seriously. "Hey, you want to see something? It's a secret. My mom and dad don't know about this."

"How can I resist?" said Anna. "What is it?"

"Just the key to popularity, that's all."

Anna raised her eyebrows. She was already pretty popular—at least she had been in junior high—but a little boost in high school couldn't possibly hurt.

Peggy set her plate on the floor. She eased herself

forward and off the bed, landing on her hands and knees. Then she turned around and reached under the mattress. "Move over," she told Anna. "You're sitting on it."

Anna scrunched over obligingly.

Peggy withdrew her hand. She offered Anna a school composition book with a mottled black-and-white cover.

Anna took it curiously.

"Go on. Open it," said Peggy, climbing back on the bed.

Anna opened the cover. At the top of the first page the name "Jenny Whitelaw" was scrawled in Peggy's round penmanship. Underneath it, written with many different pens and in many different hands, was a list of comments:

> Smartest girl in the class.
> Brains aren't everything.
> Rats on her so-called "friends."
> *No*. Only rats on her *enemies*. Jenny
>   *is loyal*.

The list went on almost until the end of the page.

Anna flipped through the book. Each page was similar, but with a different name at the top. Most were girls' names, some were boys' names. She paused every now and then to read another comment.

"Has gorgeous hair," was written under the name "Louisa Matthews."

"Thinks he knows everything," was written under "Ken Johnson."

Christine Mazur's page started off with "Says she

wears a 36B. Really wears a 34A. Stuffs cups."

Anna began to giggle. "What *is* this?" she asked Peggy.

"A slam book. You've never seen one?"

"I've never heard of such a thing."

"It's great!" exclaimed her cousin. "I started this one last January. See, what you do is pass the book around at, like, slumber parties, or in the cafeteria or during study hall. You make up a page for anyone you want— kids you like, kids you hate, cute boys, dorks, whoever. Then people write what they *really* think about those kids. You don't have to sign your name, so you can say *any*thing. There's even a page for me in there."

"Can I look?" asked Anna.

"Sure," replied Peggy. "Here, let me find it."

Anna passed the book to her cousin, and Peggy opened it to the back. She turned a few pages. "This is it," she said after a moment.

Anna peered over at the book, which lay open in Peggy's lap.

"'Peggy Wallace,'" she read aloud. "'Nice clothes . . . Snores at night.'"

"Suzanne wrote that after a slumber party," said Peggy with a giggle.

"How do you know who wrote it?"

"I can tell the handwriting."

"But I thought . . . oh, well." Anna looked back at the book. "'Tortured Mr. Bickman.' Who's Mr. Bickman?"

"He was this jerk substitute." Peggy looked rather proud of herself.

"Oh. . . . 'Funniest girl in the class. . . . Boy crazy.'"
Peggy blushed. "'Needs to—needs to lose some
weight'? That's not very nice," said Anna

Peggy shrugged. "Well, it isn't always. In fact, it isn't
usually. But it can be funny. Look at the third page in the
book."

Anna took the book out of Peggy's lap and opened it
to the third page. "Garrett Greeson," she read.

"The biggest dork ever known to mankind," Peggy
added.

Anna read aloud: "'Briefcase, slide rule, pens in
pocket, pimples on face, all present and accounted for.'"
She giggled. "'Most likely to father a geek.'" Anna
laughed loudly. "You know what, Peggy?" she exclaimed. "I want to start one of these. It'll be a way to
show I'm not just a little nobody freshman at Calvin
High. Soon all the kids will know me. . . . You *can* pass
a slam book around to upperclassmen, can't you? Or to
kids you don't know?"

"Sure," replied Peggy. "Carefully. And you've got to
be careful that the book doesn't fall into the wrong
hands. Some kids think their pages are funny. Others
don't. Garrett Greeson didn't."

Anna wasn't listening. "I'm going shopping for
school stuff tomorrow with Jessie and Randy and Paige.
I'll buy a book then."

Peggy had one last warning for Anna. "Remember,"
she said as she slid the slam book back under the mattress, "don't let your parents see it."

Chapter Two

"Mom," said Anna, "since it's the last day of summer vacation, don't you think I deserve a special treat?"

Mrs. Wallace looked skeptically at her daughter. "Exactly what do you have in mind?"

"Well, I need school supplies—"

"Honey, I gave you money this morning."

"I know," replied Anna, "and Jessie and Randy and I were going to ride our bikes over to the shopping center, but then I thought you could drive us out to the mall instead. It's so much *bigger*. It has better stores. *Please?*"

"That's *it?*" Mrs. Wallace asked after a pause. "That's all you want? I thought maybe you were going to ask for blood from a stone."

"*Mo-om.*"

"Of course I'll drive you to the mall. Call Jessie and Randy. Tell them we'll pick them up on the way."

Anna was on the phone immediately. But she used the upstairs extension for privacy. She didn't want her mother to hear the first of her three calls. It was to Paige Beaulac, whom Mr. and Mrs. Wallace didn't like. For that matter, neither did Mr. and Mrs. Taylor, Randy's parents, nor Mrs. Smith, Jessie's mother. Mr. Smith didn't care about much of anything, except his job.

"Can you meet us out there?" Anna asked Paige.

"Sure," was the casual reply. "I'll get Dwight to drive me." Dwight was the Beaulacs' chauffeur.

"Great," replied Anna. "We'll see you by the fountain. We'll probably get there around two-thirty."

Then Anna phoned Jessie and Randy, and soon she and her mother were backing out of the driveway.

"I suppose Jessie is glad school's starting again," commented Mrs. Wallace.

"Oh, you *know* she is. She can't wait."

Jessie Smith was one of the few kids in Calvin who was always glad to see school start again. It wasn't that she was a hotshot student or anything. She wasn't. She was mediocre. But school was a place to *go* to. If she got busy enough, joined enough activities, she could spend most of the day at Calvin High—from seven-thirty in the morning until five-thirty or maybe six. Evenings could be spent at the public library doing homework. Or maybe with Anna, as they often were.

Anna knew that Jessie had to be an expert at staying out of her house. It was the only way to escape the fighting. And Jack, of course.

"He ought to be put away!" Anna had once heard Jessie shriek at her father. "Jack ought to be *locked up*."

Mr. Smith had looked at Jessie with annoyance. He opened his mouth to speak, and Anna had wished that for once in his life he would be on Jessie's side, but all he had said was, "Is that any way to talk about your brother?"

Jessie had stormed out of the kitchen, followed nervously by Anna, and had invited herself over to the Wallaces', where she spent a good deal of what Mrs. Wallace called "refugee time."

"People have said a lot worse about Jack," Jessie had told Anna later that night as they were getting ready to go to bed. "Why don't my parents ever listen to them? Why don't they listen to *me?*" Then, without pausing, she had answered her own question. "Because they're too busy fighting, that's why. Honestly, you wonder what ever possessed them to get married in the first place. If my father's as big a drag as Mom is always saying, then why did she say yes when he proposed? If she'd said no, they wouldn't have gotten married and they wouldn't have had Jack and they wouldn't have had me and we wouldn't be in this mess."

Anna had stared wide-eyed at Jessie. Eight years of friendship had not accustomed her to Jessie's outbursts. Her own family was so quiet and smooth. She couldn't imagine having to share a house with the bickering Smiths, let alone with Jack.

"I wish they'd just split up," Jessie had continued ex-

plosively. "I really do. It would be better for everyone.
And I'd live with my mother, and Jack would live with
my father. Divorced families do that sometimes, you
know—divide up the kids along with the money and
furniture. Then Jack would be out of my life, and I'd
have Mom to myself, and the two of us could lead a
nice, normal, *quiet* life." Jessie paused. "Did you know
Jack was arrested last weekend?" she went on.

Anna nodded.

"Breaking and entering," Jessie had said, shaking her
head. "You know what he wanted the money for, don't
you?"

Anna knew. "Drugs."

"He's got a *prob*lem," Jessie said. "I wish Mom and
Dad would see it."

"I'm sure they do see it," Anna had told her friend,
"but they don't want to. It's like, if they don't do anything about it, then they don't have to admit there's a
problem. And who wants to admit their son's a drug
addict?"

Jessie had reluctantly agreed with Anna. For the time
being, all she could do was stay away from home as
much as possible.

Jessie was waiting when the Wallaces stopped in front
of her house. She was sitting solemnly on the low stone
wall, her long braid hanging in front of her right
shoulder. But she leaped to her feet and tossed her braid
back as the car drew up. "Hi, you guys!" she called
happily. She climbed into the back seat.

In the front seat, Anna and her mother smiled at one

another. They knew why Jessie was happy.

"On to Randy's," Anna announced.

Randy Taylor lived just two streets away.

Until fifth grade, she, Jessie, and Anna had been the very best of friends. Then the Taylors had moved to Chicago for three years. When they returned shortly before the start of eighth grade, the girls had picked up their friendship, but it hadn't been quite the same.

In Chicago, Randy had had experiences that Anna would never be able to understand fully. It was on the second day of sixth grade that Randy had first been called an Oreo. Until then, the only Oreo that Anna or Randy had known about was the cookie. When Randy had looked confused, the name-caller had said, "Oh, come on, girl. You know what an Oreo is—black on the outside, white on the inside. That's you. You're more white than black."

"I am not!" Randy had retorted. "I'm black. Look at me."

The other girl shook her head and turned away. "Like I said, black on the *out*side, *white* on the inside."

Anna thought about this from time to time; the unfairness of it all. Somehow, that comment had changed Randy's life. In Calvin, the Taylors were the only black family in the neighborhood, so Randy had grown up playing with Anna and Jessie and other white kids. In fact, the Taylors were one of the few black families in all of Calvin. The girls hadn't thought much about it, though, until the Taylors had gone to Chicago. There, Randy was thrust into a black world—except that the kids wouldn't accept her. "You're white, girl. White on the inside." Well, fine. Randy decided to seek white friends. But in Chicago, in her "integrated" school, the white kids played with the white kids and the black kids played with the black kids, and nobody wanted to play with Randy.

It had wounded her.

She'd returned to Calvin three years later—older, no taller (Randy was wiry and petite), and wary of friendships. And Anna, although she and Randy had written letters to each other sporadically, hadn't exactly spent the previous three years just waiting for Randy's return. She and Jessie had made new friends, and in fact, their closely knit group of girls had become the leaders of their class in junior high—they were the ones most of the other girls looked up to, envied, copied, tried to impress, and wanted to sit with.

Randy had fit in, though. Anna and Jessie had welcomed her back, so their friends had, too. But Randy was cynical sometimes. "Do I *really* fit in?" she'd asked Anna once. "After all, I'm black." Three years earlier that thought wouldn't have occurred to Randy. Now it was the focus of her life. Where *did* she fit in? Was she really an "Oreo"? She didn't know.

And Anna certainly didn't either. But she did know that right now she was glad to see Randy back from her family's summer vacation.

Anna smiled at Jessie and Randy in the back seat. "Mom's just taking us to the mall and *dropping us off*. Right, Mom?" she said, facing front. "Hint, hint."

Mrs. Wallace sighed. "I don't know, Anna." She glanced nervously in the rear-view mirror. "I could always stay and shop. . . ."

"Mom, what could happen to us in the mall? It's not like we're going to New York City. We know how to be careful. We'll never let go of our purses, we won't talk to strangers, we won't run naked up the down escalator."

Jessie and Randy giggled, and even Mrs. Wallace smiled. Anna breathed a sigh of relief. She was pretty sure her mother wouldn't stay. Thank goodness, because she didn't want her to catch sight of Paige.

"So, Mom," said Anna again, "you're just dropping us off, right?"

"Yes," replied Mrs. Wallace. "Against my better judgment. Do me a favor, though—stay out of the video arcade, all right?"

"Oh, definitely, Mom. No problem."

Anna and her friends hated the video arcade. It was noisy and filled with little kids. Besides, video games were passé. History.

Mrs. Wallace flicked on her right blinker and headed down the exit ramp. To the left stood Calvin Mall, a monstrosity, an eyesore . . . a shopper's dream.

True to her word, Mrs. Wallace let the girls out in the parking lot by the back entrance and, after Randy assured her that her father would pick the girls up later, drove off.

The girls entered the mall at Foreman's Department Store and walked through to the central area.

"We're meeting Paige by the fountain," Anna said.

"She should be there already. We're a little late."

"I can see the fountain and she's not there," said Randy.

"Well, let's sit down. Maybe she's off 'shopping.'"

Anna and Jessie began to giggle and were still laughing as they settled themselves on a bench to wait for Paige. Randy remained silent. They all knew Paige wasn't off shopping. She was off shoplifting, which never failed to make Randy angry.

Paige turned up shortly, a big shoulder bag in tow.

"Been shopping?" Anna couldn't help asking.

More giggling.

Beautiful Paige perched on one end of the bench, and the other girls inched over to make room for her.

"I got here early," replied Paige. "I've been shopping for almost an hour."

"Oh, God," said Jessie. "Is there anything left?"

"What'd you get?" asked Anna.

Paige looked in both directions before opening her shoulder bag.

"Do you have to show us here?" asked Randy. "Couldn't this wait until we're outside?"

"If you're chicken," replied Paige huffily, sitting back and starting to close the bag, "I can—"

"Oh, come on," said Anna. "Jessie and I aren't chicken. We want to see, don't we, Jessie?" Anna flashed an annoyed look at Randy.

But Randy wasn't about to give in. "I'm going to the stationery store," she said. "I'll wait for you guys in there."

Paige made a face at Randy's retreating figure. Then she opened the bag. She pulled out a sweater, a pair of earrings, a belt, a credit card case, and a tube of body glitter.

"How much did you pay for all this stuff?" asked Jessie.

Paige smiled. "Four dollars. I had to buy the body glitter. It's from Fiona's, and they watch you like hawks in there. The other stuff came from Hurley's. You could walk out of there with an elephant and no one would notice."

Anna and Jessie giggled.

Paige's smile remained pasted across her face. "Well, let's go meet Randy before she turns me in," she said.

Anna sighed. She wished Paige and Randy got along better. They were both part of "the group," but they had never hit it off. Despite Randy's attitude, though, Anna admitted (only to herself) that Paige was really the one at fault. She knew that Paige considered Randy worlds apart from her.

The Beaulacs lived in a mansion, the biggest home in Calvin. It wasn't even near Anna and Jessie and Randy's neighborhood. Mrs. Beaulac had hired two people to keep the house running—a cook/housekeeper and a gardener/chauffeur. Anna knew Paige was convinced that Randy ought to be jealous of her. Randy, however, led a "normal" life with two parents and a sister who loved her. The Taylors weren't divorced, and there were no drinking problems over at 1252 Linden Lane. Nevertheless, Paige was sure that deep down Randy wanted a life like the Beaulacs'. A fancy name and a big house and people to wait on her. Her own credit cards with unlimited spending.

Anna, Jessie, and Paige found Randy browsing through the stationery store, her arms loaded with notebooks and pens and paper and reinforcements and dividers, and all sorts of things Paige couldn't be bothered with. One spiral notebook was enough for her.

"You're getting *all that?*" Paige asked her. What she was really saying was, "If I had as little money as you, I certainly wouldn't waste it on school supplies."

Randy ignored the unspoken question. "Yeah," she said. "My parents always give Tanya and me some money for school stuff at the beginning of the year."

"How sweet," muttered Paige, but only Anna heard her.

"I want to get off to a good start in high school," Randy went on. "I'm going to make my mark at Calvin High. Scholastically, that is."

Paige turned away. "I'm going to make my mark at Calvin High," she mimicked softly. She headed for the notebook aisle while Randy took her supplies to the cash register. Paige had made her mark at a total of five schools—four private schools and Calvin Junior High. CHS would make the sixth.

Mrs. Beaulac had had no intention of sending Paige to public school, but Paige had been tossed out of every private school in the area. And her year at a boarding school, in fifth grade, had been a dismal failure. Her mother's only choice was to send her daughter to the

Calvin public junior high. And that was where Paige had transferred just after Christmas during seventh grade, and met Anna.

Paige flounced down the notebook aisle, picked up one notebook and one Bic pen, and got in line at the cash register behind Randy. Anna had never seen her shoplift. It was something she would do only when she was by herself.

"Are you guys finished already?" Anna called to Paige and Randy from around a display of lunch boxes.

"Yeah, but take your time," replied Randy. "We don't mind waiting."

Anna returned to the notebooks. Her arms were full, and she already had a notebook for every subject she'd be taking, but she hadn't found the one she most wanted —a composition book with a splotchy black-and-white cover like the one Peggy had pulled out from under her mattress the day before.

Jessie appeared at her elbow. "Ready?" she asked.

"Almost." Anna glanced at Jessie's pile of supplies. "Hey, where'd you find that?"

"Over there," replied Jessie, pointing.

Anna turned. Behind her were the composition books. *Slam books,* Anna told herself with a smile. She picked one up. "Now I'm ready," she said to Jessie. "Come on, let's go."

When the girls left the store clutching their bags, Anna thought, *Ready or not, Calvin High School, here we come.*

Chapter Three

On the morning of her first day in high school, Anna was up early, nervous and excited. She was determined to make a good impression on the upperclassmen, so she changed her clothes three times before she decided she was wearing an outfit that was neither too babyish nor too matronly, too plain nor too punk.

Randy rang the doorbell early that morning, and Anna rushed to meet her.

"I'm so nervous!" they said at the same time. They laughed.

"You look great," Anna told Randy. "How many times did you have to change before you put that outfit together?"

"Three," replied Randy as they set off.

"Me too," said Anna. "Oh, Randy, what are we getting ourselves into? *High school.* We're going to be lowly little freshmen. We won't even know most of the kids in our own class since they'll come from the other junior highs. And it's true about the upperclassmen and the lipstick and freshman hazing. Hilary came home with a big red *F* marked on her forehead after her first day at CHS. And we don't know our way around. I don't even remember where the office is."

The previous spring, all the eighth-graders in Calvin had been taken on tours of the high school building. It had seemed vast and imposing to Anna. She remembered nothing of the layout, only a blur of staircases, halls, and doorways. From the outside, the building looked like a medieval fortress. Inside, it seemed like a maze.

"Hey, there's Jessie. Jessie!" Randy called.

"Hi!" replied Jessie, grinning broadly. She was running across her front lawn, notebook tucked under one arm, purse over the other, braid flying. "At last!" she exclaimed. "School is finally here! The summer is *over.*"

Randy shook her head. "I like school and all that," she said, "but you're amazing."

"Well, you know," Jessie replied vaguely.

"Yeah," said Anna and Randy. They knew all too well.

"So what are we waiting for?" said Jessie. "Let's get going. I've been waiting for this day since June twenty-third."

When they reached the high school, Anna searched

the campus. "Paige said she'd wait for us out front, but I
don't see her."

At that moment, a long silver Cadillac pulled up near
the front door of the school. A door opened. A black
man in a uniform got out. He walked to the back door
and held it open while Paige Beaulac slithered out, her
notebook in hand.

"What time shall I return for you?" Anna could hear
Dwight ask.

"Oh, three o'clock, I guess." Paige didn't even look
at him. She spotted Anna, Randy, and Jessie and ran
over to them. "Oh, I am so *embarrassed*," she exclaimed. "Why do I have to start school like this? Everybody's *looking*." Paige's face was flaming.

"If he could just have let me off on the side street,"
Paige went on. "Even that would have made a difference." Paige sighed. "Can you believe Mother's in Europe again?" she said grumpily. "She's never around for
anything important in my life."

And when she is around, Anna thought, *she's usually
drunk*. Anna wondered how Mrs. Beaulac had managed
to win full custody of Paige in the bitter battle that had
followed the Beaulacs' divorce.

Anna looked at the kids beginning to trickle into the
building. "Hey, we better go!" she said.

"What's the big hurry?" asked Paige.

"The big hurry is that we want to find our homerooms
before it gets too crowded in there. The fewer people
who see us wandering around, the better."

The girls walked to the main entrance and edged inside. Ahead of them was the school trophy case, cups and plaques and team photos proudly displayed.

"It's kind of exciting, isn't it?" said Randy in a hushed tone.

"Yeah, but you don't have to whisper," replied Paige. "This isn't a mausoleum."

The girls turned right and walked along a dim, noisy corridor until they came to an intersection.

"Now what?" whispered Jessie.

They pulled out their schedule cards, as if the cards would provide directions to the rooms.

I hate *this*, thought Anna. *Talk about bottom of the heap.*

"Randy and I have to get to the second floor," said Jessie. "And there's a staircase. We better take it."

"We'll see you guys at freshman lunch," added Randy.

"Okay," said Anna.

"See you later!"

"See you later!"

The girls parted. Anna and Paige looked around.

"Hey, we're standing right in front of my homeroom!" Paige said suddenly.

"I guess I'm on my own, then," Anna replied, her knees beginning to feel shaky.

"Good luck," Paige whispered. She ducked into the classroom.

Anna stood in the middle of the intersection. Students buzzed around her. She was just about to choose a direction randomly, when she felt a hand on her shoulder.

She turned and found herself looking into a hand-some, concerned face. "You look kind of lost," the boy said.

All of Anna's defenses crumbled. "I'm looking for room one-eighteen," she told him.

The boy frowned. "One-eighteen," he repeated slowly. "Oh, yeah! That's down on the plaza level. Go downstairs, turn right, and go past the metal shop. It's one of the rooms on the intersecting corridor."

"Thanks," said Anna. "I'd never have found it."

"No problem," said the boy. "And good luck."

Anna smiled at him. Then she turned and headed for the staircase. Maybe high school wouldn't be so bad after all.

The lower level was much quieter than the main floor. In fact, Anna didn't see any students at all. Neverthe-less, she turned right and began looking for the shop. She passed the boiler room—and came to a dark dead end.

He must have meant left, not right, Anna told herself.

She retraced her steps, reached the stairs, and kept going. She turned several corners, found the offices of the coach and the school dietitian, and a room full of computers—but no classrooms.

When she heard the warning bell ring, she began to panic. It was slowly dawning on her that she'd been tricked. Where was that staircase? Anna rushed around a corner and found stairs, although not the ones she'd come down. She ran up them anyway and emerged on the noisy ground floor.

For a moment, she stood stock-still.

"Excuse me. . . . Ex*cuse* me," said a harried voice behind her.

Anna stepped aside to let the person behind her pass by, and bumped into a red-haired girl who was leaning against a locker talking to two friends.

"Hey!" the girl exclaimed.

"I'm sorry, I'm sorry," said Anna. Then she screwed up her courage and asked the way to room one-eighteen.

"Right over there, through the boys' room," said the redhead.

Anna felt her face burn. She began to walk away.

"Hey, come back," called one of the girls.

Anna turned around hopefully.

"We don't give information away for free, you know," said the girl.

"But you didn't—"

"The price is clean shoes." The redhead handed Anna a tissue and pointed downward.

Anna looked around in desperation. The halls were beginning to clear out, but the next bell hadn't rung.

"What're you waiting for? Christmas?"

Slowly, Anna stooped down. She set her notebook and the slam book on the floor and began shining the girl's shoes. After a few seconds, the girl said, "That's enough."

Anna picked up her books. As she was straightening up, a hand reached out for her face. Anna saw the lipstick tube and felt the three quick strokes.

"Have a nice day, freshman!" called the red-haired

girl. She and her friends hurried down the hall just as the second bell rang.

"This is terrific, this is just terrific," Anna muttered. "Now I'm late." She reached up to daub at the lipstick on her forehead and realized that she was standing in front of the door to her homeroom.

She heaved a sigh that was relief mixed with humiliation, and went inside.

The cafeteria at CHS was as noisy and as crowded as the hallways were between classes. Anna and Paige, who had run into each other in the corridor, stood at the entrance, scanning faces for Jessie and Randy.

Anna was almost afraid to go in. She was not used to feeling unsure of herself, and she didn't like it. She was supposed to be Miss Popularity, not Miss Invisibility.

Anna felt someone brush by them. "Hi, Paige," said an airy voice.

The voice belonged to Casey Reade, who waltzed past Paige with a grin on her face and Gooz Drumfield on her arm.

Paige smiled sweetly. "Hi, Gooz," she said pointedly.

"Hey," Gooz replied vaguely.

Griswald Drumfield had been *the* most gorgeous boy in junior high school. His blond hair curled just slightly, his deep-blue eyes always sparkled, and his even white teeth smiled at the world from a deeply tanned face. Gooz was rich (though not as rich as Paige), smart, and athletic. If he was a bit quiet, nobody noticed, particularly not Paige, who, Anna knew, had set eyes on Gooz

on her first day in public school and had never taken
them off him. Gooz, however, had shown no interest in
Paige, and Casey had snagged him at the end of eighth
grade.

Paige made a face, and Anna groaned inwardly. This
could be trouble. Paige had never liked Casey much anyway. She said Casey was too cute.

Anna followed Paige through the cafeteria. And at last
she caught sight of Jessie. She ran to her. "Boy, am I
glad to see you. . . . Oh, you got lipsticked!" she exclaimed.

"So did you!"

"Yeah. Where's Randy?"

"On the lunch line," said Jessie. "Let's sit over there.
See that empty table? Go put your stuff down, and we'll
get on the line before it's too long."

When the girls were settled at their table and had
begun their lunches, they compared notes on the morning's injustices.

"I didn't get lipsticked," said Paige, "but a bunch of
boys blocked my way and made me late for algebra."

"I got lipsticked *twice*," said a morose Randy, who
sported one *F* in the middle of her forehead and another
over her left eye. "It's not fair."

Anna listened to their stories. She looked around at
her friends isolated at the small table in the middle of the
bustling cafeteria. In their junior high, where they had
known almost everyone in their class, the four of them
were the center of attention at lunchtime. Here they
didn't know two-thirds of the kids, and their former

classmates were busy simply trying to recover from the morning and find niches for themselves in the strange environment.

Suddenly, Peggy's words came back to Anna. *The key to popularity.* Anna was holding it in her lap. She peeked down and could see the black-and-white blotches looking back at her. They were practically calling to her.

When she couldn't stand it any longer, Anna shoved her lunch tray aside and opened the slam book in front of her.

"What's that?" asked Paige.

Anna explained.

Her friends were fascinated, and Paige was the first to suggest a name to go in the book. "Casey Reade," she said, with a look of great satisfaction.

And that was how the slam book was started.

Chapter Four

The first day of school began no differently for Cheryl Sutphin than any other day. It barely mattered to her that she would be going to Calvin High School instead of junior high. And it certainly didn't matter to her father.

Bud Sutphin was snoring away in the other bedroom. The house was tiny enough and the walls thin enough so that Cheryl, still lying in bed, could tell that Bud had tied a really good one on the night before. She knew because booze snoring is different from regular snoring.

Cheryl rolled over. No alarm clock had awakened her. Her body could tell somehow when it was six-thirty, and signaled her every morning—weekday, weekend—without fail. She sat up and got heavily to her feet.

Cheryl felt nothing, absolutely nothing, about starting at CHS. She wasn't nervous, wasn't excited. She merely figured that her status at school wouldn't change substantially. She'd been fat, friendless, and unaccepted in elementary school and junior high. She didn't see why high school should be any different.

Cheryl put on her green dress. It had once been a housecoat belonging to her mother. After her mother had died and Cheryl had gained even more weight, she had remodeled the housecoat to make it suitable for school. It hung limply, straight from her shoulders, but Cheryl managed to spruce it up a little by pinning on her mother's peacock brooch and tying a bathrobe sash around her waist as a belt. It was the best she could do, but she couldn't really tell how she looked since the only mirror in the Sutphin home was on the medicine chest in the bathroom, and it had cracked ages ago. Bud would never scrape together the money to replace it.

Cheryl put on a pair of sneakers, forgot to brush her hair, and tiptoed into the dark kitchen. The light was busted in the refrigerator, but it didn't matter. Cheryl knew the contents: half a quart of milk, a package of baloney, a package of Wonder Bread, a six-pack of orange soda, two six-packs of beer, and an apple. In the kitchen cabinets were marshmallows, Oreos, Jell-O mix, and some cereal.

Cheryl added milk to a bowl of Captain Crunch and helped herself to two Oreos. When her breakfast was eaten, she listened at her father's door. The booze snoring had stopped, but he wasn't stirring.

Cheryl crept outside to wait for the school bus. She steeled herself for the jeers that would begin as soon as the driver opened the door.

Chapter Five

Somehow, Anna survived the rest of the week at CHS. The lipsticking stopped after the first day, and the maze of hallways began to make sense. She was still uneasy about the sea of unfamiliar faces, freshmen or otherwise, but at least a few more of last year's big group had joined her lunch table—and Peggy had been right. The slam book did attract kids. Anna told a few people about it, and they told a few people, and *they* told a few people. . . .

Nevertheless, that first week was tough. Everything at CHS was new; nothing was familiar. So when Paige suggested a slumber party at her house on Friday night, Anna jumped at the idea.

"Oh, great!" she exclaimed. "You, me, Jessie, and Randy? Perfect!"

"Well . . . yeah," agreed Paige, and Anna knew that she hadn't intended to ask Randy. But Anna would never leave Randy out.

Anna had to do some fast talking to get permission to go to Paige's, though, and her mother didn't give in until Friday morning.

After school that day, Anna threw together a bag of things to take to Paige's—a Lanz nightgown, her makeup case, her hairbrush, her toothbrush, and a bottle of shampoo. Then she packed one last item.

The slam book.

She laid it reverently on top of her nightgown.

The slam book was beginning to look used. One corner had been bent. Some of the white splotches had been doodled in. Anna looked at it fondly before zipping her duffel bag closed.

Mrs. Wallace pulled into the circular drive in front of the Beaulacs' just before five-thirty. Anna kissed her mother goodbye, then ran to the double front doors and lifted the brass knocker. She watched her mother swing out along the drive and, as Paige answered the door, realized that Mrs. Wallace was glancing in the rear-view mirror, watching the house swallow her daughter up.

Paige had asked Anna to come over early to help her with the party, but by the time Anna showed up, nearly everything was ready. Two spectacular pizzas had been ordered, the refrigerator was stocked with every soft drink anyone could ask for, music was playing on the compact disk player in Paige's bedroom, Paige had selected a stack of movies for the VCR—and Mrs. Beaulac was working on her third martini.

"Mother," said Paige, "don't you think you've had enough to drink? At least for now?"

The elegant Mrs. Beaulac, seated stiffly in the formal living room of the big house, crossed her legs and set her glass down with a clunk on the antique end table. "Please do not start with me, Paige," she said. "It was a long flight home. I have jet lag. I need to unwind."

This did not make a bit of sense to Anna. Having jet lag meant you were tired. And alcohol relaxed you, slowed you down. Drinking seemed to be exactly the wrong thing to do for jet lag. Besides, it wasn't as if Mrs. Beaulac's plane had just landed.

Apparently, Paige was having similar thoughts. "But Mother, you got home yesterday," she pointed out.

"I still have jet lag."

Anna shifted from one foot to the other, wondering if she should wait in Paige's room. Mrs. Beaulac had acknowledged Anna's presence with a tiny wave and had then seemed to forget about her. Anna finally decided it would be rude to leave.

"Mother, if you're tired, why don't you go to your room?" suggested Paige, trying a different tactic. "Savanna left dinner. I could bring you yours on a tray later. You could eat in bed with your TV on or something."

Mrs. Beaulac smiled thinly. "Don't think I can't see through you, Paigie. You're afraid I'm going to embarrass you. You're afraid I'm going to say something in front of your friends."

Paige squirmed. She glanced at Anna, who took a

step backward. "Mother, just please—"

"Oh, for heaven's sake. I'm going to be on my best behavior, okay? Scout's honor." Mrs. Beaulac raised two fingers. She giggled giddily.

Paige shook her head. "Come on," she said to Anna. "Let's put your stuff upst— No, wait. I have an idea."

"What?" asked Anna, but Paige didn't reply. She ran back to the kitchen. Anna followed, watching as Paige found a bar guide and looked up "martini."

"Gin and vermouth," Paige muttered.

"Hey," said Anna. "I'm not going to drink—"

"Fine," said Paige. "More important, neither is Mother."

Paige snapped the book shut, replaced it, and went to the liquor cabinet. She removed several bottles of gin and vermouth and stashed them under the utility sink in the pantry.

"There," said Paige. "That should do it."

Randy was the next to arrive at the Beaulacs'.

"Did you bring the slam book?" was the first thing she asked, even before she had set her gear in the hallway.

"I've got it right here." Anna patted her duffel bag, which she had left in the lavish foyer. "Hey, I hope you're hungry."

"Starved," replied Randy.

"Great. Because Paige ordered two super-size Pizza Giants."

"Pizza Giants!" exclaimed Randy. "You ordered from Pizza Giant? All *right!*"

Paige managed a small smile. "They're supposed to

be delivered at seven. Where's Jessie?"

"She'll be here soon. She stayed after school for a meeting of *The Tower*. She's decided she wants to write for the paper," Randy said.

Anna shook her head. "In a few weeks she'll be playing lacrosse, singing in the choir, working on scenery for the drama club. Anything to stay out of her house. We'll never see her."

"She's crazy," Paige muttered.

"She is n—" Randy began hotly, but was silenced by a look from Anna. The look meant *Don't start anything.*

"Let's go to your room, Paige," Anna suggested. "We need to dump our stuff somewhere."

Paige's room was spectacular. That was the only word for it. Like the rest of the house, it was huge. At one end was a working fireplace. Nearby was a brass canopy bed. The wall-to-wall carpet was so deep and fluffy, Anna was sure she could sink right through it into the kitchen below. A wall of shelves held Paige's books and videos, her television set, VCR, the compact disk player, and rows of stuffed animals and collector's dolls that Paige hadn't looked at in years.

It was a dream room.

Anna flopped back and said, "Should we read the slam book now or wait for Jessie?"

"Better wait for Jessie," Randy replied. "She'll kill us if we start without her."

"You're right," said Anna. "By the way, I passed it around in my biology class this afternoon. Mr. Morris was late, so everyone at my lab table was writing in it."

"How many names now?" asked Paige. The girls had started with nine on the first day of school—their own, plus Casey Reade, Gooz Drumfield, Dale Rice (supposedly the smartest girl in their class), Ben Cooperstein (star football player), and shlumpy Cheryl Sutphin, the loser of their class—dumpy, not too bright, and a terrible dresser.

"Twenty-four," Anna replied promptly. "You've seen how the kids flock to this thing. It's like the slam book is honey—and they're flies."

"Yoo-hoo!" a tipsy voice called up the stairs. "Yoo-hoo! Paigie, you're little friend ish here!"

Paige's cheeks flushed hotly, and she leaped off the bed. Before she had reached her door, her mother appeared, leading Jessie by the hand.

Mrs. Beaulac rattled the ice in her glass and, for no apparent reason, burst into a fit of giggles. Jessie pulled her hand away and dashed into the bedroom, shooting a pained look at Paige. "I have a meshage," said Mrs. Beaulac, still giggling. She ran a hand through her frowzy hair. "Your peetsha ish here and your friend ish late. . . . No, that'sh wrong. Your peetsha'sh late and your friend'sh here. Right here. Ash a fatter of mack, I mean, a matter of fack . . . heeeere'sh Jeshie!"

"Oh, Mother," murmured Paige.

Mrs. Beaulac slumped against the doorjamb and smiled drowsily at the girls. She let her glass tip to the side, and the melting ice cubes sloshed onto the rug. "Shorry. Don't know what the troblem is . . . prouble is . . ."

"Mother, did Pizza Giant call?" Paige asked wearily.

"I just shaid sho, didn't I?"

"Not exactly." Paige looked apologetically at her friends. "I'll be back in a minute," she told them. "I better check on the pizzas."

Since Paige had a phone in her room (her own private line), Anna knew that what Paige really wanted to do was put her mother to bed, or do whatever it is you do for a drunk person.

When Paige was gone, Anna, Jessie, and Randy looked at one another with raised eyebrows.

"Mrs. Beaulac even *smells* drunk," Jessie whispered.

Randy made a face.

"I haven't seen her this bad in a long time," remarked Anna.

"We better not talk about it. Paige'll be back any minute," said Randy. "I'm going to put something on the VCR."

Randy turned off the CD player and selected a movie from the stack. By the time Paige returned, the girls were laughing hysterically over *Ghostbusters*.

The slam book remained shut, waiting in Anna's duffel bag, until *Ghostbusters* was over and the Pizza Giants were as eaten as they were going to get. When the empty boxes had been thrown away, the leftover slices wrapped and put in the refrigerator, and the girls settled on Paige's bed, Anna finally opened the slam book.

"Are you ready?" she asked the others.

They nodded nervously.

"Whose page should we read first?"

"Oh, let's just start at the beginning and go through," said Paige.

"Read our own?" asked Anna, her voice squeaking. "Out *loud?*"

"Let's look at our own last of all," Jessie suggested. "Just open to any old place."

So Anna closed her eyes and selected a page. "Gooz Drumfield," she announced, a little shiver running through her body, leaving goosebumps on her arms. She was glad she was wearing a long-sleeved shirt. "'What a hunk,'" she read. "'Gorgeous . . . Stuck up.'" She looked at her friends. "I don't think he's stuck up. Maybe a little shy. Oh, well. That's just somebody's opinion." She continued with, "'Cutest boy in the entire world.' . . . Hey, Paige, is that your handwriting? It looks like it."

Paige blushed. "Of course not," she replied quickly.

"See what's on Cheryl Sutphin's page," Jessie suggested, suppressing a giggle.

Anna flipped backward through the book. "'Cheryl Sutphin . . . Buys clothes at the Salvation Army.' . . ."

"That's not very nice," Randy interjected.

"'She isn't playing with a full deck,'" Anna continued. "'Possible head lice?'" (Hysterical giggling from Paige and Jessie.) "'Lose a ton or two, Cheryl! . . . Shops in "mature women's" department . . . Once broke my camera just by posing.'"

Even Randy laughed at that comment.

"I can't stand it any longer," said Anna. "I've got to

see what's written on my page—but in private." She carried the book into Paige's bathroom.

Anna took a deep breath, let it out slowly, then perched on the toilet seat. As the keeper of the slam book, she'd been tempted many times to look at her page, but she hadn't been able to bring herself to do it.

I could not *look,* she thought, *and just pretend I did*.

She sat for a few more moments. Then in one decisive movement, she snapped the book open, whizzed through the pages until she came to her own, and forced herself to read:

> All-around nice girl.
>
> Little Miss Popularity.
>
> Has beautiful eyebrows.

Anna shot up and examined her eyebrows in the mirror. They *were* kind of nice.

She returned to the book.

I wish I were more like her.

Boy! thought Anna. There was nothing like that written about Peggy in *her* slam book.

Anna read on, feeling pleased with herself.

> Popular, pretty, cool.

Anna was positively glowing!

She emerged from the bathroom, smiling. "Not bad," she told the others. She hadn't cared for the phrasing of "Little Miss Popularity," but she really didn't have anything to complain about.

"My turn!" Paige exclaimed. She also carried the book into the bathroom. When she returned, she was not smiling.

"Well?" said Randy.

Paige looked thoughtful. "I don't agree with everything, but—hey, we can add to the slam book any time we want, can't we?"

"Sure," replied Anna.

"Perfect. I'll just show Miss Casey Reade how it feels to be insulted."

"What are you talking about?" asked Jessie.

"Here, look." Paige thrust the slam book at the girls.

They peered at Paige's page. It started off with the usual comments about her looks ("Too perfect," "Most beautiful girl in the class"), her money ("Share the wealth, Beaulac!"), and her personality ("Snob," "What an ego").

"I can take all that," said Paige, "especially 'Most beautiful girl in the class.'" She grinned. "I hope a boy wrote that. This is what I'm talking about."

The last entry on the page was rather long and was written in shaky letters.

"Allow me to read it for you," said Paige. "'What's next, Beaulac? Reform school? Or couldn't your mother get you in there, either? Good luck following in her footsteps. Maybe you'll graduate from CHS with a double degree in drinking and shoplifting.'"

"Jeez," said Randy. "Who would write stuff like that? Hey, Paige, you don't really drink . . . do you?"

"I will not dignify your second question with an answer," replied Paige stiffly. "As for the first, obviously Casey wrote it."

"Casey?" said Anna. "Why?"

"Because she hates me, that's why. Because she knows I like Gooz, and she feels threatened."

Anna took the book from Paige and looked closely at the comments. "I really don't think Casey wrote that. It's not anything like her handwriting."

"She disguised it," said Paige matter-of-factly. "And I'm going to pay her back. Let me have the book."

Anna handed it over.

Since Paige's handwriting was distinctive—angular and slanted, with quirky flags on the *k*'s and *l*'s—she got a special pen from her desk and, in beautiful calligraphy that looked nothing like her usual penmanship, wrote at the bottom of Casey Reade's page: "What a liar. Everyone knows you didn't *really* do it with Gooz."

"Paige!" exclaimed Randy with a gasp. "She never said . . . *that*."

Paige shrugged. "She might have."

Jessie began to giggle. "I think it's kind of funny. It's just a joke anyway, right?"

"Sure," said Paige. "Listen, I'm going to get us something to drink. That pizza made me thirsty. I'll be right back."

Anna and Randy glanced at each other. Very slowly, Anna picked up the slam book, closed it, and put it in her duffel bag.

"Wait!" cried Jessie. "Randy and I didn't get to read the stuff on our pages."

Anna handed Jessie the book.

Jessie began to read silently. After several seconds her face grew red.

"Jessie?" asked Anna.

Jessie swiped at her eyes. Then she closed the book and threw it against a wall.

"Hey!" said Anna.

Without a word, Jessie ran into the next bedroom, gathered up her gear, and started down the staircase.

"Jessie! Where are you going?" cried Randy. She and Anna ran after her.

"Home," Jessie replied briefly. "Don't worry, I'm not going to walk. I'll call my mother."

"I'll do it for you," said Randy. She dashed back to Paige's room.

As Jessie and Anna were running down the staircase, they met a bewildered Paige on her way up with a tray of sodas.

"What's going on?" she asked.

And it was then that Anna was sure she smelled liquor on Paige's breath.

Chapter Six

When Mrs. Taylor dropped Anna at her house the next morning, Anna dumped her duffel bag inside the front door and shouted hello and goodbye to whoever might be at home.

"Where are you going, sweetie?" called her mother from the kitchen.

"Over to Jessie's. She left the party early last night."

"Everything all right with her?"

Anna stuck her head in the kitchen. "Actually, I don't think everything *is* all right."

"Oh, dear. Poor Jess," said Mrs. Wallace. "Invite her over for some refugee time if she needs it."

"Okay," replied Anna. "Thanks, Mom." She dashed out the front door.

Anna was two houses away and across the street from

the Smiths' when she heard the fighting.

She paused, feeling a wave of nausea. Then, slowly, she crossed the street.

The screaming grew louder. It was coming from the second story. Anna could make out separate voices.

"You keep your face out of my business!" That was Jack. Anna could picture him standing in his bedroom, which was more like a garbage dump.

"Young man, as long as you live under this roof, your business is my business. Where have you been? Kids your age do not stay out all night." That was Mr. Smith.

"I called last night, didn't I?" Jack shouted. "What else do you want?"

"First you call to tell me you're not coming home. Ten minutes later, some woman I barely know calls to complain that you and God knows who else are hanging around her house corrupting her son. Then you don't show up here until noon today."

"Corrupting her son! That pothead—"

"Shut up! Shut your mouth. I don't want to hear—"

Anna shivered. She had never heard her own father tell anyone to shut up. She'd never even heard him raise his voice.

There was a pause in the fighting.

Then Mr. Smith's voice could be heard again. "You stay out of this!"

Who? Who did he mean? Jessie?

"What's the matter, Dad? 'Pot' is a dirty word, huh?" It was Jack.

"You're damn right it's a dirty word."

"It's so dirty that practically every kid in school uses it, and a lot of other stuff. Ever heard of crack, Dad?"

"Ever heard of the police?" Mr. Smith shouted back.

More silence. Anna bit at a nail.

Jack was notorious at CHS for his drug use. At least, so she'd heard. As far as she knew, he hadn't been at school those first days. Of course, he was over sixteen. He was dropout age.

But really. Anna agreed with Jessie. If the Smiths couldn't see what was going on with Jack, they were blind. Jack had lost weight. He was wired and jumpy and nervous as a cat. He couldn't hold still for a second. Whenever Anna saw him, his hands were moving and his feet were tapping. According to Jessie, he was never home for a meal. He lived on Twinkies and cupcakes and potato chips. His room was a wasteland of crumpled-up wrappers, cookie crumbs, half-empty Coke cans. Once last spring, Anna had arrived earlier than usual at the Smiths' to walk to school with Jessie, and there was Jack stumbling around the house, swaying if he tried to stand still, gazing at Anna from red, hooded eyes. He smelled as if he hadn't showered in weeks.

The silence in the Smith home was shattered by a shriek and the sound of glass breaking.

Anna shrieked herself. It was time to alert her parents. But she hadn't run more than a yard when she heard the Smiths' front door slam. She hesitated. If it was Jack, she wanted to get out of there. But if it was Jessie . . .

She turned around.

"Anna!"

"Jess!"

"What are you—" Jessie began to say at the same time Anna said, "I was coming over to see—"

They paused to catch their breaths.

"I was coming over to see if you were okay," said Anna. "But I can—I mean, I heard . . . you know. . . . "

"It's World War Three in there," said Jessie, her voice quavering. "I was on my way to *your* house. I had to get out of there."

"I don't blame you. Listen, I heard something break." Anna looked nervously over her shoulder at the house. "Are they okay? Do you think we should call—"

"No!" cried Jessie. "We shouldn't do anything. Just go to your house, that's all."

"Okay, okay." Anna took Jessie by the hand, trying to comfort her wordlessly, but the farther the girls walked, the more upset Jessie became. By the time they reached the Wallaces', Jessie was crying so hard she could barely speak.

Mrs. Wallace must have been watching for them from a window. As soon as they reached the front stoop, she opened the door, put an arm around Jessie, and led her inside.

Over cups of tea, Jessie's story emerged. The fight had started when Jack had come home that morning, having been out all night.

"Dad gets mad at Jack," said Jessie, "and then he gets mad at Mom. I'm not sure why. He hardly ever gets mad at me, mostly just ignores me." Jessie sipped her tea, slowly gaining control of herself. "I feel so bad for

Mom. Her whole life is Dad. Cooking for him, keeping house for him. He's such a pain. Everything has to be just so, in place, in order. And boy, she better be ready to entertain if Dad says he's bringing home clients or something. It's like he's a—a dictator." Jessie flushed. Her eyes met Anna's over the rims of their teacups.

Anna flushed, too. She knew where *dictator* had come from. She'd read Jessie's page in the slam book to see what had upset her so much the night before. And she'd found it, a sarcastic comment in handwriting that, oddly enough, looked something like Paige's: "Meet the Smiths, the all-American family—Hitler, Houdini, Cinderella, and the addict."

Hitler was Mr. Smith, the dictator. Houdini was Jessie, the escape artist. (She *did* run away from her problems.) Cinderella was Mrs. Smith. And the addict, of course, was Jack.

"The thing is," Jessie went on, "Mom knows Jack has a problem. Well, anyway, she thinks he's difficult. But she won't do anything about it because she says my father wants to handle Jack his own way. It's like she's afraid to do anything on her own."

"Would your mother like to have a job, Jessie?" Mrs. Wallace asked suddenly. "It would be a part of her life that's separate from your father."

"Oh, she'd never try to get one," replied Jessie. "But she *would* like to have one. You know what she's trained for? Interior design. She says she used to be pretty good. She also says that if she got a job, my father would divorce her."

Mrs. Wallace raised her eyebrows.

"Which is funny, because I wish he *would* divorce her."

The talking continued until dinner. Jessie decided to spend the night at the Wallaces'. She hadn't brought any clothes over, but it didn't matter. She could borrow Anna's.

Anna didn't think of the slam book again until after she and Jessie had gone to bed that night.

Hitler, Houdini, Cinderella, and the addict. The words came back to her. Anna envisioned them on the page. And she envisioned the look on Jessie's face when she'd read them.

For the first time, she felt a twinge of doubt about the slam book.

Chapter Seven

"Anna, have you got it?"

"Where is it?"

"I have to show Polly something. She won't believe this!"

Three girls pounced on Anna the moment she walked into the cafeteria on Monday. They were three of the most popular girls from Summit Junior High.

Grinning, Anna pulled the slam book out from between her notebook and her history book. "It's right here. Come on." She led the way to a much larger table than the one she, Randy, Jessie, and Paige had slunk to on their first day at CHS.

The girls took the slam book and hustled to one end of the table. Anna sat at the opposite end, saving seats for her friends, who showed up shortly. The girls who had taken the slam book were squealing, groaning, and laughing.

"Aughh! 'Wears her underwear inside out'!"

"'Prettiest girl in Ms. Fox's homeroom.' Thank you! Thank you!"

"Anna, where's the slam book?" Two breathless girls ran over to Anna's chair.

"Hi, you guys," said Anna. "It's down there. With that boy next to Charmaine Kroll."

The girls rushed to the other end of the table. "I'm coming with you," Paige called after them. "I want to see something."

Paige abandoned her half-eaten lunch and made a dash for a seat near Charmaine.

Anna looked at the table with great satisfaction. Close to twenty kids were now crowded around it, wolfing down sandwiches and poring over the slam book. This was the way things should be, she thought. She and Jessie and Randy and Paige were the center of attention again, or at least connected to the center of attention, which was actually the slam book.

Even the kids who weren't sitting at Anna's table seemed drawn to it. One was Cheryl Sutphin, eating alone as usual. She was wearing a faded, shapeless housedress that she must have made herself. Her father, who held various odd jobs, earned barely enough money to pay the bills, so Cheryl was forced to cut corners wherever she could. Judging by her weight, however, she didn't cut many corners when she went grocery shopping for herself and her father. Cheryl gazed at

Anna's crowd while she slowly ate a mayonnaise and baloney sandwich on a hamburger bun and drank a Coke.

Not far from Cheryl, a group of completely unfamiliar, mousy-looking girls watched Anna's crowd enviously.

And not far them *them* was another lone figure, only she had turned her back on the cafeteria and was looking out the window while she ate.

The figure was Casey Reade. . . . Wasn't it?

Anna nudged Randy. "Is that Casey over there?" she whispered.

"Yup," replied Randy grimly.

"What's she doing alone? Where's Gooz?"

"Didn't you hear?" asked Randy. Randy glanced at Paige, now engrossed in the slam book with the others, then turned back to Anna.

"Hear what?" asked Anna.

"Yeah, what?" added Jessie, turning away from another conversation.

"Casey and Gooz broke up this morning. They had a big fight," said Randy.

"You're kidding!" Jessie exclaimed. "It must have been over what Paige wrote in the slam book. Remember—about Casey not really . . . you know . . . doing it with Gooz." Jessie blushed.

"No way," said Anna. "How could that get around so quickly? Paige wrote that on Friday night. It's only Monday."

Randy shrugged. "Who knows? Paige probably made

one phone call to one person and happened to mention what she wrote—although not the fact that *she* wrote it. That would do the trick."

"Wow," whispered Anna.

"Hey, there's Gooz!" Jessie was peering toward the far entrance to the cafeteria.

The girls watched as Gooz edged around tables, hands in pockets, unsmiling.

"Maybe he's going to talk to Casey," suggested Randy.

But Gooz walked by Casey. He bought a sandwich, walked by Casey again, and approached Anna's table.

"He's coming over here!" squealed Anna.

"What do you bet he sits next to Paige," said Jessie. "I'm sure she managed to plant a rumor about herself, too. Something intended to attract Gooz."

Gooz, sandwich in hand, pulled a chair up next to Tim Skelly, a football friend of his, and the two started a quiet conversation.

From across the table, Paige watched them solemnly. After a few moments, she edged closer to them. She lowered her eyes so that her long lashes kissed her cheeks. Then she glanced up at Gooz.

"Gooz?" she said softly.

Gooz looked as if he didn't hear her, although he faltered in his conversation with Tim.

"Gooz?" Paige said again.

"Yeah?" He finally turned toward her.

"Gooz, I wanted to tell you how *sorry* I was to hear about you and Casey. That's just awful."

"Well . . . thanks," said Gooz. "Listen, I really don't want to talk about it. Okay?"

Before Paige could answer, Gooz returned to his conversation with Tim.

Paige looked wounded. But not for long. "Gooz," she said, this time breaking right into the discussion, "did Carson assign your class any homework for tonight? I just can't—"

"Paige, listen, if you don't mind, I'm trying to talk to Tim."

"Oh. Excuse *me*." Paige turned away in a huff and flounced back to the end of the table.

Gooz and Tim shook their heads.

'Wow," said Anna to her friends. "Did you see that?"

"Pretty interesting," commented Jessie.

"I had a feeling Gooz didn't like her," added Randy, "but I didn't think he felt *that* strongly about it."

"You knew Gooz didn't like her?" Anna whispered. "How come you didn't say anything on Friday when she was going on about Casey feeling threatened by her?"

"What was I supposed to say?" Randy whispered back fiercely, her eyes flashing. "She barely tolerates me as it is. She thinks I ought to clean her house, not visit it."

"Randy!" Anna exclaimed with a gasp.

"Well, it's true, isn't it?"

Jessie shrugged, and Anna mumbled, "I don't know," but they both knew it probably was the truth.

For several moments, none of the girls spoke. Randy finished her lunch, crumpled up her sandwich wrapper, and deposited it neatly in her milk carton. Anna and

Jessie mechanically spooned lukewarm tomato soup into their mouths.

"Pretty quiet down at this end of the table," said a deep voice.

Anna looked up to see Gooz Drumfield moving to the chair next to hers. He smiled at her with his toothpaste-commercial teeth.

"I guess we're all talked out," replied Anna, trying to laugh.

"I don't believe it," said Gooz. "Three beautiful women all talked out?"

"Ooh, you're treading hard on the thin ice of the women's movement," teased Randy.

Anna saw that Randy was smiling and knew that she wasn't really angry, at least not at Anna or Jessie.

"But go ahead and tread," added Jessie. "Flattery will get you everywhere."

Gooz settled into the chair, and his smile faded.

"We're, um, sorry about you and Casey," Jessie said quietly.

"Yeah, well . . ."

"Gooz . . ." said Anna slowly, aware that he had told Paige he didn't want to discuss the subject and not knowing where her nerve came from, "don't you think that rumor was just, well, a rumor?"

Gooz flushed.

"I mean, I don't know. What did Casey say when you asked her about it? Did she say she had really been telling people that you . . . you know?"

"She denied it," said Gooz flatly, "but that's not the

point. It was the way she reacted when I confronted her. She just blew up. It started this big fight about our entire relationship. We would have broken up sooner or later, anyway. I guess."

Anna nodded sympathetically, feeling guilty at the same time. Maybe they would have broken up, and maybe not, but Paige had seen that they did—and Anna could have prevented it.

"Listen," said Gooz, leaning close to Anna, "I was wondering—"

"Well, I better be going!" said Jessie suddenly. "Come on, Randy."

"Right!" answered Randy, too quickly. "I wanted to—to show you—"

"Whatever," Jessie supplied. She grabbed Randy's elbow and hustled her toward the trash cans so they could empty their trays before they left the cafeteria.

"That was subtle," Gooz commented, and Anna giggled.

"Anyway," he went on, "I was wondering if you'd want to work on that history project with me. Mrs. Seifert said we could either work alone or in teams. I don't have any ideas, but the proposal isn't due for two weeks. You want to try working together?"

"Sure!" exclaimed Anna. "I haven't come up with an idea yet either, but together maybe we could think of something really good."

Anna felt like singing. Gorgeous Gooz was paying attention to *her*. Incredible! But her elation vanished when her eyes met Paige's at the other end of the table.

In one moment—so short a time that Anna wasn't sure she had actually seen it—Paige's eyes flashed pure hatred at Anna. Then Paige stood up and stalked out of the cafeteria.

Bewildered, Anna turned back to Gooz. Apparently he hadn't noticed. The bell rang, and Anna tracked down the slam book and tucked it between her books again. Gooz walked her to her next class. Although neither Anna nor Gooz was aware of it, both Casey and Paige followed them through the halls, staring at them angrily.

Chapter Eight

Cheryl's baloney sandwich was sitting in her stomach like a rock. She had eaten it too quickly, but she didn't mind. For once she'd had a really good seat in the cafeteria. She had been alone, as usual, but near enough to the table that Anna Wallace, Jessie Smith, Paige Beaulac, and that Black girl, Randy somebody, shared. They were the popular kids—at least they had been in junior high—and they fascinated Cheryl. Especially Paige. No doubt about it, Cheryl and Paige were true and exact opposites. Paige was the richest girl in Calvin; Cheryl was the poorest. Paige was fair and beautiful; Cheryl was blotchy-skinned and homely. Paige was willowy; Cheryl was fat. Paige was smart; Cheryl was . . . well, not. The list went on and on.

Today the girls had been passing around some kind of

book. Everyone wanted to see it. They read it, wrote in
it, squealed and laughed over it, and one girl looked like
she'd cried over it. It must be really something, that
book. Whatever it was.

Cheryl patted her unhappy stomach. She crossed and
uncrossed her legs. Study hall was the l-o-n-g-e-s-t class
teachers had ever invented, especially when you didn't
have much to do. Which Cheryl didn't. She looked
around her. This study hall room was bigger than any of
the ones at the junior high school. There were forty,
maybe fifty kids in it.

A flurry of activity caught Cheryl's eye. Over to her
left, something was being passed secretly from student
to student, lap to lap. That was the only way to do it,
Cheryl thought. The only way to pass something all the
way across the room without getting yelled at by the
study hall supervisor.

Cheryl watched the progress of the something. Closer
and closer it came. Cheryl seemed to be right in its path.
Now it was two students away from her, now one. The
boy on her left—a complete stranger—slipped it to
Cheryl and indicated that she should pass it along.

What an honor! Cheryl was never included in good,
secret things like this. She'd do her part, all right. She'd
pass it—

Cheryl paused mid-pass. She drew in her breath. It
was that book. *That book.* The one everyone had been
looking at during lunch. It was right in her hands.
Cheryl slid her eyes to her left and her right. The kids on
either side of her were silently begging her to keep the

book moving. But Cheryl was safe. The kids couldn't really do anything without getting caught.

Cheryl opened the book. It looked like a regular old notebook, except that the pages had been written in by lots of people. Different handwritings, pencils, blue pens, red pens, a green pen. At the top of the first page was the name "Casey Reade." The things written under it must have been about Casey. There were comments like "Showoff," "Casey and Gooz, the perfect pair," and "Needs a bigger bra. Ha ha." Cheryl blushed. That kind of talk wasn't nice. Hadn't her mother always told her so?

Cheryl turned the page. The next few pages were like the first, but with different names at the top.

There was a page for Paige Beaulac. Paige's page! That was a pretty funny joke, thought Cheryl. Her mother would have liked it. She'd always liked Cheryl's jokes.

Cheryl studied the page. "Too perfect," "Most beautiful girl in the class," and "What an ego" were a few of the comments. Hmm.

Cheryl turned another page. Her own name jumped out at her. There it was. Right there. "Cheryl Sutphin," it said. "Buys clothes at the Salvation Army." How did they know? Cheryl wondered. She'd only done that once. Who had been watching her?

"She isn't playing with a full deck." Cheryl frowned and read on. "Possible head lice?" *Head lice?* Cheryl didn't have head lice. What a rotten thing to say. "Lose a

ton or two, Cheryl." A deep flush crept up Cheryl's neck
to her face.

"Once broke my camera just by posing." It took
Cheryl a moment to figure out what that meant. When
she did, tears slowly filled her eyes.

Cheryl skipped to the last comment on the page. It
read, "Her mother isn't dead, she's in the wacko ward."

That did it.

Her mother had been dead for five years. And her
dying hadn't been easy. It had taken a long time, and it
had hurt a lot. Why would someone say Cheryl's mother
was crazy? That just wasn't right.

The tears spilled over, and Cheryl was ashamed.

She slammed the book onto her desk. It slid to the
floor.

As Cheryl gathered up her things, the kid on her right
grabbed for the book.

The study hall supervisor called after Cheryl as she
ran out of the room, but Cheryl ignored her.

From her desk in the corner, Anna watched the whole
scene. As Cheryl fled, Anna closed her eyes and slowly
shook her head.

Chapter Nine

The next day, Anna and Randy were the first to reach their table in the cafeteria.

"Where's Jessie?" asked Randy.

"Trying out for the orchestra. She's coming later."

Smiling, Randy shook her head.

"Tomorrow," Anna continued, "the poetry review. The next day, gymnastics." Anna unwrapped her tuna fish sandwich. "So don't you want to know what happened with Gooz yesterday?"

"Of course I want to know. I'm dying to know."

"He asked me to be his partner on the history project!"

"Hey, great!" exclaimed Randy.

"What do you think it means?"

"Well, it—"

"It could mean that he's an awful history student and wants my help," said Anna, answering her own question. "Or it could mean that . . ." Anna lowered her voice and glanced around. "Do you think this is Gooz's way of saying he's interested in me? And if he *is*, what does that say about him? Yesterday, he was still going out with Casey. Is this what people mean by 'catching someone on the rebound'? Or maybe he's even trying to make Casey jealous."

"Oh, God!" exclaimed Randy, giggling. "Why don't you just take it at face value for now? He asked you to work on the history project and that's all. So work on it with him. Don't worry about what it might or might not mean."

"You're right," Anna agreed.

"Where *is* Gooz?" Randy asked.

"He said he had to talk to his math teacher this period."

Anna sensed that the kids were going to start asking for the slam book, so she pulled it out of her notebook.

"Hey, let's read Gooz's page!" she said suddenly. She began to thumb through the book, but it fell open to her own page. Anna's attention was drawn to a new comment on the very last line. In Paige's spiky penmanship was written, "Gooz's next conquest? How far will she go?" Above that, in printing she didn't recognize, was written simply, "Boy-stealer."

"Hey!" exclaimed Anna.

Boy-stealer! She was not! Who had written that? But Paige's comment was more disturbing. Paige hadn't even bothered to disguise her handwriting. What had gotten into her?

"Look at this," said Anna indignantly. She pointed out Paige's comment to Randy.

Randy frowned. "That was pretty stupid of her. She knows you'd recognize her handwriting. What's wrong with that girl?"

"Well," said Anna thoughtfully, "she *has* been pretty cool—ever since Casey and Gooz broke up and Gooz started paying attention to me."

"But that wasn't your fault," Randy pointed out. *"Paige* was the one who suggested that Casey and Gooz 'did it.'"

"Keep your voice down," said Anna. "Look who just got here."

Paige was pulling out a chair at the opposite end of the table. She was as far away from Anna and Randy as she could get.

"What's Paige doing way down there?" Randy whispered.

"Sulking," a voice answered. It was Jessie. She plopped down next to Randy. "She's been in a real mood lately."

Anna snapped the slam book shut.

Well, sulking was one thing, but damaging people's reputations was another. Didn't Paige know that everyone saw what was written in a slam book? Sooner or later, Gooz would see the remark, too.

Then it hit her. Of *course* Paige knew that would happen.

Boy, thought Anna miserably. *Paige must really be angry with me. How unfair! She created the mess, and now she's trying to hurt me. Some friend she is. Well, Paige Beaulac, two can play your game.*

The only problem was, Anna wasn't very good at certain games, and now that it was her turn, she had no idea what move to make.

The problem, however, was cleared up that evening.

While Anna and her parents were eating dinner, the telephone rang.

"I'll get it!" Anna exclaimed, jumping up so fast she startled Bucky.

"If it's for you, keep it short," Mr. Wallace cautioned.

"Okay."

Anna picked up the phone in the kitchen and walked away from the dining room, stretching the cord to its fullest length.

"Hello," she said. "Wallace residence."

"Hello . . . Anna?"

"Hi, Gooz!" Anna recognized his voice right away. She reached down to ruffle Bucky's fur. He had followed her into the kitchen after recovering from his fright.

"Hey! How are you? Am I interrupting dinner or anything?"

"Well, actually we are eating, but I can talk for a minute."

"Geez, you eat late. It's seven-thirty. How do you make it from freshman lunch until seven-thirty?"

"Snacks," replied Anna. "And plenty of them."

Gooz laughed. "You look too thin to be a snacker."

"Looks are deceiving."

"Sometimes."

What kind of conversation was this?

"So . . ." said Anna.

"So," said Gooz, "I was wondering if you'd like to get together Friday night. I know it's short notice, but the movie at the Playhouse just changed. You want to go?"

"Sure!" replied Anna. She didn't even care what the movie was. For Gooz, she'd sit through a documentary on golf tournaments, if necessary.

"Great. My brother and his girlfriend are going, too, so they can give us a ride. We'll pick you up around six-thirty. Is that okay?"

"It sounds perfect," said Anna, who wasn't even sure her parents would let her go out with a boy.

"Great," said Gooz. "And how about working on the history project after school tomorrow? We've got to hand the proposal in soon."

"That's fine," replied Anna. "But I better check with my mother and father about Friday. Can I call you back tonight?"

"Okay. I'll talk to you then."

"Okay. And thanks! 'Bye, Gooz."

"'Bye."

Mr. and Mrs. Wallace were not at all happy to hear about Gooz's invitation—at first. But Anna was ecstatic about the call and couldn't stop smiling as she pleaded with her parents. Finally they gave in, on the condition that Anna be home by ten. She decided she could live with that.

"You know, honey, you look positively radiant," Mrs. Wallace told Anna after she got off the phone with Gooz later that evening. "It's amazing what a little attention can do. The Pygmalion effect at work."

"Oh, *Mom*," Anna said.

But her mother's words gave her the idea for her next move in the game with Paige.

Thank you for your handwriting, Anna silently told Paige as she retreated to her room and pulled the slam book out of its hiding place in her closet. *It's a good thing everyone in our entire class can recognize it. You want embarrassment, Beaulac? I'll give you embarrassment.*

Anna opened the slam book and studied several comments written by Paige. Then, on a pad of scrap paper, she practiced writing in Paige's scrawl until she could do a decent imitation. When she was ready, she turned the slam book to Cheryl Sutphin's page, and in Paige's hand wrote, "If only Cheryl knew how much Kirk Norris likes her, maybe she'd fix herself up."

It was a serious move in a dangerous game.

Chapter Ten

Gooz walked Anna to the library after school on Wednesday. The sidewalk felt like clouds under Anna's feet. She couldn't believe that she'd been in high school only a week, and already she was one of the most sought-after girls in the freshman class. *And* Gooz Drumfield was at her elbow. It was all thanks to the slam book.

One way or another.

Just the sight of the slam book made her shiver—a little thrill of delight and fright, of pleasure and fear. She felt the shiver when she read flattering comments about herself, or when kids crowded around her, asking for the book. She'd also felt it when she'd watched Cheryl Sutphin discover her page in the book, and when she'd painstakingly written "Paige's" comment on Cheryl's page later that night.

Anna put the slam book out of her mind, though, so that she could enjoy Gooz and her cloud-walk to the public library.

"So," said Gooz. "Tell me about you. I mean, tell me the things about you that I don't already know."

Anna blushed. She could never think of interesting things to say about herself. She cleared her throat. "Well, um, I'm the baby of our family. My sister Hilary's married and has a little boy."

"So you're an aunt," said Gooz with a smile. "Aunt Anna."

"Yeah. Only Seth—that's the baby—calls me Aunt Annie. And I'm going to be an aunt again in January."

Gooz nodded. "What else?"

"I like to read."

"What else? Tell me something deep and personal."

"I feel like I'm at the shrink's!" said Anna. "I don't know what to say. . . . Oh, here's something. I'm a Leo."

Gooz laughed. "That wasn't quite what I meant."

"Well, give me a clue. Tell me about you," said Anna.

"Okay," replied Gooz. "Let's see. I'm very organized. And very neat. Clutter drives me crazy—unless it's under the bed where I can't see it. I say what's on my mind. And I'm very honest."

"How honest?" asked Anna.

"Incredibly honest."

"If a store clerk was making change and accidentally

gave you a ten-dollar bill instead of a five, would you tell him?"

"Yup," said Gooz.

"What if he gave you a quarter instead of a nickel. Would you tell him?"

"Yup."

"What if the store was all the way over in Greendale, and you didn't realize the mistake until you got home?"

"Are we talking about the quarter or the ten-dollar bill here?" asked Gooz.

"The quarter."

"I guess there's a limit to my honesty."

Anna and Gooz walked on, smiling.

"Any ideas about the project?" asked Gooz as they approached the library.

"Just a time period," replied Anna. "I like the Second World War. But let's not do anything about Hitler and the concentration camps. Everybody chooses those topics."

"Something to do with American life during World War Two?" suggested Gooz.

"Yeah, that's good. Hey!" exclaimed Anna. "I wonder if we could find enough information right here in town to do something about Calvin during World War Two."

"How about the effects the war had on a typical small American town?"

"Oh, that's perfect! We can interview people who lived here then. And maybe the library has copies of the *Calvin Chronicle* from the thirties and forties."

"Yeah! Seifert's going to love this!"

Anna entered the library in great excitement—at least, with as much excitement as she ever felt about a school project.

An hour and a half later, she and Gooz left in just as much excitement. The library had the *Calvin Chronicle* on microfilm dating back to 1932 and two books about Calvin written by local historians. Furthermore, Anna realized that anyone fifty or over would remember at least something about the war. There must be plenty of native Calvinites over fifty whom they could interview.

The most exciting thing about the afternoon, however, was what happened after Gooz had walked Anna to the corner where they would have to separate.

"I'm glad we've got this project under way," Gooz said.

"Yeah, me too," replied Anna.

"And I'm really glad we're working together." Gooz gazed seriously at Anna with his china-blue eyes.

Anna actually thought she might keel over on the sidewalk. She didn't think she'd ever seen eyes as intense as Gooz's. She was sure they could see into her very soul.

"Oh, me too," replied Anna, recovering herself.

"Well, catch you in school tomorrow."

Gooz leaned down and kissed Anna on the forehead. Then he turned and strode off.

Anna was dumbstruck. She practically flew home. She ran through the front door, dropped her books on the floor in the living room, called hello to her mother, and dashed to the upstairs phone.

She dialed Randy's number. No answer.

Anna had to tell *some*body. She took a chance that Jessie might be home, and dialed the Smiths.

After five rings, Anna was ready to hang up. It was so frustrating! She had this fabulous news—and no one to tell it to. The receiver was almost back in its cradle when Anna thought she heard a click. She jerked the phone to her ear.

"Hello?" said a voice. It sounded like Jessie . . . but not quite.

"Jessie?" asked Anna.

"Yeah?"

"It's *me*. I've got major news!"

Silence.

"Jessie? Are you there?"

"Yes." Jessie's voice was fading.

"What's going on? Are you okay?"

"My mom just left."

"Left for where?"

"Left for good," said Jessie. "Walked out. Took a hike. Set herself free." Jessie's voice was rising hysterically.

"Calm down," said Anna sharply. "Are you alone?"

"Aloner than ever." More giggling.

"Come over, Jess," said Anna. "Mom and I are here."

Jessie's giggles turned to sobs. "What am I going to *do*, Anna? She *left* me. I always thought she'd leave *them*, but not *me*. I thought I'd go with her. We belong together. . . . She *left* me."

"Jess, come *over* here. Right now. Please. Okay?"

"Okay, okay, okay."

Anna ran downstairs. "Mom," she cried, "Mrs. Smith walked out. Jessie's, like, hysterical or something. She's coming over here. Let me talk to her alone first, all right?"

"Oh, dear God," said Mrs. Wallace. "Yes. All right. Why don't you and Jessie go to your room? I'll come upstairs a little later."

Anna nodded. She forced herself to be calm. When the doorbell rang a few minutes later, she answered it immediately, hugged Jessie, and escorted her upstairs.

"Jess, tell me everything that happened, okay?" she said as they settled themselves on Anna's bed.

"Yes. Okay." Jessie drew in a deep breath. "Okay," she said again. "I came home early. I was supposed to go to a meeting this afternoon, but it was canceled. I went to my parents' room, and I saw these two suitcases open on the bed. They were overflowing with clothes. And Mom was pulling stuff out of her drawers and the closet.

"So I said, 'Where are you going? What's wrong? Is Grandma sick? Or Grandpa?' And Mom said, 'No, no, they're both fine.' Then she handed me this piece of paper and said 'Here, read this. I was going to leave it on your dresser.' And then she started trying to close the suitcases."

"What did she give you?" asked Anna.

"This note." Jessie thrust it toward Anna.

"Dear Jessie," the note said. "I don't know where I'll be by the time you read this. I can't live with your father anymore. I have to get out and start a life of my own. I know you'll understand. I promise to write to you often. If you want to get in touch with me, call Grandma and Grandpa. They'll know where to reach me. Everything will work out one day, Jessie. I promise. Remember that I love you. Mom."

"Oh, my God," was all Anna could say.

"I didn't know what to do," Jessie went on. "For some crazy reason, all I could think of was this scene from *Mary Poppins* where little Michael Banks is just staring at his nanny, and Mary Poppins tells him to close his mouth because 'We are not a codfish.'"

Jessie giggled nervously. "So my mother is, like, bustling around the bedroom. She'd closed the suitcases, but she kept finding things she wanted to add to them. Photographs and stuff. And I just *watched*.

"Finally Mom looked around and couldn't find anything else to pack. So I actually helped her lug the suitcases downstairs. Then she called a cab and asked to be taken to the train station. She sat on that wooden bench in the front hall, waiting.

"I started to say something, but Mom said, 'Don't make me say anything. I can't say anything. The note says it all. One more word, and I won't be able to leave.' I should have said another word." Jessie rubbed her eyes. "Then the cab came and Mom kissed me and left. And then you called. I haven't even told my father yet."

At that moment, Mrs. Wallace knocked softly on Anna's bedroom door and let herself in. Jessie burst into tears. Anna's mother sat on the bed and rocked Jessie back and forth until her sobs subsided.

Five minutes later, Mrs. Wallace called Jessie's father at his office.

Chapter Eleven

Jessie stayed with the Wallaces for two nights. Then Mr. Smith ordered his daughter home. "He doesn't want *me*," Jessie told Anna and Randy the following week. "He wants a cook and a maid. It's too bad he can't afford real ones, but he's used to my mother, who worked for free."

Jessie was angry, but Anna was glad for it. Her friend was returning to her old self. She'd been depressed and melancholy since her mother had left. And now with Jessie back at her house, Anna could begin to concentrate on other subjects—like Gooz and the history project. Their proposal had been accepted, Friday night had been wonderful, and Gooz had asked her to go out with him again on Friday.

Anna had agreed immediately. Going to the movies

the week before had been an experience she knew she'd never forget. If you didn't count going to the library, then Friday had been the first time Anna had ever gone out with a boy, and she had felt very special. It wasn't because Gooz did things for her, such as hold doors open and buy her popcorn (although he did); it was that Gooz made Anna feel that no one and nothing else was as important to him as she was then. She found herself the center of someone else's universe. It was scary, but it was also exhilarating.

Then there was the slam book. The kids who had seen "Paige's" comment about Cheryl Sutphin had taken it for a joke. Nobody, including Paige, could figure out who'd written it. Anna didn't know what Paige thought about the joke, though, since Paige barely spoke to her anymore. Or to Randy or Jessie, for that matter. Anna supposed this was because they were still friends with Anna. Any friend of Anna's seemed to be an enemy of Paige's.

Anna had selected Kirk Norris as the object of the slam-book comment on Cheryl's page for a specific reason. He was not the most popular boy in the freshman class, but it was generally agreed that he was one of the *nicest*. He was polite, funny, smart, and involved in school activities. He could always be counted on to lend a hand. Almost every kid in the class knew him and liked him, despite the fact that he wasn't particularly good-looking, wasn't a sports star, and certainly wasn't any Romeo. Kirk was a good choice because he didn't have a girlfriend, but he was the kind of guy a girl would be flattered to be liked by.

On Friday Anna managed to position herself near Cheryl in study hall. She came in a little late, giving Cheryl enough time to get settled, and sat down at one of the many empty desks surrounding her. Anna worked studiously for twenty minutes. Then she asked the supervisor for permission to leave the room to get a book out of her locker. She left the slam book open on her desk, turned to Cheryl's page, and angled it toward her. She figured that no matter how hurt Cheryl had been, she wouldn't be able to resist *that* kind of temptation.

"We're going out again tonight," Anna told Randy and Jessie at lunch that day.

Gooz was sitting nearby with Tim and two other boys. He had told Anna that he didn't want to ignore his friends just because he and Anna were dating sometimes. He said he had made that mistake with Casey, and it had almost cost him his friendship with Tim. Anna respected that. She didn't want to hurt her friendships, either.

Randy grinned. "That's great. What are you going to do?"

"Movies again," replied Anna.

"Again? Did the one at the Playhouse change already?"

"No, that'll be there for years. We're going to the library. They're having a Marx Brothers festival. We're going to see *Duck Soup* and *Horsefeathers*—I think. I don't know much about the Marx Brothers, but Gooz likes them. And on Sunday we're going to work on our history project."

"I heard from my mom," Jessie said suddenly.

"What?" said Anna, her mind on Gooz.

"I heard from my mom. Last night."

"Oh, Jessie! That's wonderful!" said Randy.

Jessie shrugged.

"Well, did she call you or what?" Anna wanted to know.

"I called her. She won't call our house because she's afraid my father will answer the phone. But he was out last night, so I called my grandparents, and they gave me a number where I could reach my mom. Guess where she is."

"Where?" asked Anna and Randy at the same time.

"New York."

"New York *City?*" exclaimed Anna. "God, when she leaves, she really leaves." Randy kicked Anna under the table. "I—I thought she was going to stay with your grandparents," Anna went on, trying to be more tactful.

"Me too. But she's really getting away from things. She said she's having a great time. Maybe she just needs a break. I don't remember the last time she took a vacation."

"Well, what did she say exactly?" asked Randy.

"She said New York is huge and exciting and she loves the Metropolitan Museum of Art and she misses me. And loves me."

Jessie's eyes filled.

"Well," said Anna helplessly.

Randy reached over and took Jessie's hand for a moment. "You'll see her again," she said.

"I know," Jessie replied, sniffling. "It's just that I always thought she'd take me with her."

"You *always* thought?" Randy repeated.

"It's like, deep down, I've known all along that she'd have to get out someday. But I thought our whole family would split up, like in a divorce. I didn't think she'd just leave me."

Anna and Randy glanced at each other. They didn't know what to say. Their parents rarely even argued. Anna tried to imagine living with the knowledge that one day, one of her parents would have to leave. She couldn't do it.

"We're here," said Anna finally. "You've got us."

"And *me*. Don't forget about *me*," said a bitter voice several seats away.

It was Paige.

"I'd be de*light*ed to help you."

Anna was taken by surprise. Nobody knew what to say.

Paige shook her head in disgust, gathered up her books, and left the cafeteria.

"What's with her?" asked Jessie, bewildered, wiping her eyes. "Did I do something?"

"Yeah, you committed a federal crime," Anna answered sarcastically. "You remained my friend."

"And mine," added Randy. "Two strikes against you. You're hanging out with criminals. One of us has the audacity to be the girl Gooz went after when he dropped Casey. The other has the audacity to be black—and happy with it."

Jessie widened her watery eyes. "Whew. Big time," she commented.

Chapter Twelve

For the first time in she didn't know how long, Cheryl Sutphin woke up and nearly purred with pleasure. She rolled over in bed and stretched like a contented cat.

That book had said that if only Cheryl knew how much Kirk Norris liked her, she'd fix herself up. Well, Cheryl was going to do just that.

And Cheryl knew who'd written the comment. It was Paige Beaulac, of all people. Cheryl recognized her handwriting immediately. See? Cheryl wasn't as stupid as everyone thought.

Cheryl had had some luck. Bud was working all weekend. He had a job hauling a load of something all the way to western Ohio for a friend of his. So Cheryl had been on her own.

First thing, as soon as Bud was gone, Cheryl had

found that box of her mother's stuff—the one labeled "Veronica" that contained all of Mrs. Sutphin's things—and had gone through it. She'd found her mother's beautiful pink prom dress, the one with the filmy flowers sewn onto the sleeves and the waist, and even some old makeup.

Cheryl tried the dress on. It fit pretty well, considering. Then she experimented with the makeup. A smear of blue eye shadow here, a gash of red lipstick there. It did make a difference. Then Cheryl tried putting her hair up. She hadn't washed it in a while. Maybe it would look less dirty piled on her head. She stuck some bobby pins in to hold it in place and decided she looked older. "I hope I look half as beautiful as you, Ma," she said softly.

Cheryl would make her grand entrance at school on Monday. That is, if she could sneak out without Bud seeing her.

Cheryl's luck held out. Bud hadn't come home from his trip by Monday morning. (He was probably drinking away his earnings in some roadside bar.) Well, fine. That gave Cheryl the freedom to put the pink dress on just right and get her hair and makeup all fixed. She could sneak out without Bud's ever knowing she'd been into the Veronica box.

"Ma, stay with me today, okay?" Cheryl pleaded silently as she waited for the school bus.

Cheryl caused a stir in school, no two ways about it. When she entered Mr. Roscoe's English class, every head turned toward her. She heard rustlings and saw kids whisper to each other—even though they were supposed to be taking a test. Cheryl noted with special pleasure that Anna Wallace saw her. Since Anna was a friend of Paige's, she'd be sure to tell her that Cheryl had paid attention to what Paige had written.

Still pleased with herself, Cheryl apologized to Mr. Roscoe for being late, accepted her test paper, and sat down at her desk. She knew every eye was on her.

She'd never felt better.

Cheryl's incredible luck continued to hold out. Right after English class, who should she run into but Paige Beaulac! Paige was at her locker, hurriedly exchanging books.

Cheryl rushed over to her. "Oh, *Paige,*" she said. "How can I ever thank you?"

Paige glanced up with a look that Cheryl couldn't quite read. She must have been very surprised at the "new" Cheryl.

"Ex*cuse* me?" said Paige.

"I wanted to thank you." Cheryl reached her hand out toward Paige's arm, and Paige jerked back. She slammed her locker shut and spun the dial of the combination lock. Her face was turning red.

"Don't you know for what?" Cheryl continued.

"No," snapped Paige, backing away.

"For letting me know about Kirk."

"Great, great." Paige rushed off.

Cheryl was mystified, but she didn't give up. At

lunch, she approached Paige again. She pulled up a chair and sat down next to her.

"So what do you think?" she asked. "How did I do with the makeup?"

Paige stared at her food, apparently trying to ignore her.

"Too much lipstick?" asked Cheryl.

Paige slammed her sandwich down and walked out of the cafeteria.

Cheryl followed.

Anna Wallace was uncontrollable. She laughed for five minutes. This was the ultimate in humiliation for Paige.

That night, while she was supposed to be finishing her homework, Anna opened the slam book to Cheryl's page and in the carefully practiced spiky handwriting wrote, "What a change! I'm so proud of Cheryl! Kirk may ask her out."

Chapter Thirteen

Two new comments appeared in the slam book.
    On Anna's page:
        Sweet on the outside, evil on the inside.
        Pretty to look at, but Do Not Touch. A
        rattlesnake. *Boy-Stealer*.
    On Randy's page:
        Black on the outside, white on the inside.
        A human Oreo. Ha, ha.

    Both were in Paige's handwriting.
    Anna was fuming. How did Paige dare to write such
things? How did she even *think* of them? And why
didn't she bother to disguise her handwriting? Anna
couldn't understand the perverse pleasure that Paige
must be getting from what she'd done. Okay, so maybe

she had reason to be mad at Anna because of what had happened with Gooz. But Randy hadn't done anything to Paige. Not a thing. Yet Paige had written the cruelest, most hurtful thing about Randy that she could think of. Somewhere, far back in Anna's mind, a little alarm bell began to go off. The bell was signaling something about Paige being deeply troubled. But Anna didn't listen to it. She ignored it because she was so angry. She had had enough.

Anna brought the slam book with her to lunch. The best kind of confrontation would be a public one.

Anna arranged herself with Randy, Jessie, Gooz, and Tim at one end of their usual table. Paige was sitting at the opposite end. Anna had told no one what she was going to do. In fact, she wasn't precisely sure herself.

After a while, the slam book was taken from her pile of books and passed around. Anna kept her eye on it, as if it were a nut in the shell game. Eventually, Paige reached for it.

Almost without thinking, Anna rose from her seat and walked to the other end of the table. She snatched the slam book out of Paige's hands.

"Hey!" cried Paige. "What are you doing?"

"This is off-limits for you from now on," Anna said.

"What are you talking about?"

"Keep away from the slam book."

Paige bristled. "I'll write in it if I want to."

"No," said Anna firmly. "It's mine. And I want you to leave it alone."

By that time, all heads at the table had swiveled toward Anna and Paige. Gooz half rose from his seat.

"What's the matter?" asked Paige. "Can't take a little criticism?"

"You go way beyond criticism," Anna retorted. "You're cruel and you *lie*."

"Won't Goozie protect you?"

"Leave Gooz out of this!"

"Hey, Anna?" said Gooz tentatively.

"It's all right," Anna replied without looking at him.

"Anna, a slam book *is* a slam book," said Randy. "Anyone can write in it."

"Maybe," replied Anna, "But . . . well, let me give you a little selection of Paige's comments." Anna opened the book and thumbed through it. "Here's a nice one. This is from your page, Randy. 'Black on the outside, white on the inside. A human Oreo. Ha, ha.'"

At the other end of the table, Randy's frown turned to astonishment. She buried her face in her hands.

"And this is from my page—twice," Anna continued. "'Boy-stealer.' What a laugh. It's as funny as 'human Oreo.' And you know what's funnier?"

"Anna," said Gooz, "I think you've said enough. Why don't you put the slam book away?"

"No. I'm not finished. The best is yet to come, and I want everyone here to know about it."

Not only was Anna's table dead-quiet by then, but so were several tables nearby. Half the freshman class was listening to Paige's humiliation.

Paige, as white as a sheet, looked like a cornered animal. Her hands shook and she bit at the nail of one pinky, but she didn't move from her seat.

"What's funnier," Anna continued, "is that Paige wrote the comment that broke up Gooz and Casey. And she invented the whole thing."

"You little liar!" cried Paige. "I did not! It's not written in my handwriting! Any fool can see that."

"It's not written in your usual handwriting," said Anna, "but it's in your disguised handwriting. And you know perfectly well who will back me up on this." Anna looked down the table at Randy and Jessie.

Both girls glanced from her to Gooz. Did Anna really want them to confess right in front of Gooz?

"We were all with you, Paige," said Anna. "You wrote it, and you admitted you made it up. Am I right, Randy?"

Randy didn't answer. Anna couldn't even guess at what was going through her mind.

"What's the matter, Oreo?" Paige taunted her. "Can't talk? Miss Goody Two-Shoes can't make up her mind?"

The silence following that was louder than any Anna had ever heard. The heads, which had swiveled to Paige, now swiveled—slowly—back to Randy.

Randy stood up. "Yes, Paige wrote it and she made it up," was all she said. She began to gather her books together.

Then Jessie stood up. "What Randy is too polite to say," she said, "is that Paige wrote that, hoping it would break up Casey and Gooz. She wanted Gooz for herself."

"Thanks a lot, Jessie," said Paige sarcastically.

"Any time," replied Jessie. She followed Randy out of the cafeteria, leaving Anna and her mess behind.

"Is that true, Anna?" asked Gooz quietly.

How had the situation gotten so out of hand? What had happened? Anna had set out to show Paige for what she really was and had ended up telling Gooz the one thing that was capable of hurting their relationship. What would Gooz think of her? She'd known all along how the comment about Casey had originated, and she hadn't said a thing—especially not after she and Gooz had started going out.

"Anna?" asked Gooz again.

"Yes," Anna admitted. "It's true."

Gooz shook his head. Then he too gathered up his things. Before he left the cafeteria, he said, "I don't know who you girls think you are, but believe me, you're not God. God shows a little mercy."

"Nice going, Anna," Paige said softly, as Gooz disappeared into the hall, followed by Tim.

"Oh, shut up, Paige," Anna snapped.

"Permanently, please," added a sickeningly sweet voice from the next table. Anna turned to see Casey Reade. "You're a real witch, Beaulac. You know that? But you're not too bright. Your plan backfired nicely."

How long the fight would have gone on was anybody's guess, but it was ended by the bell. When it rang, Casey stared at Paige a second longer, then turned and marched off.

Anna made her way numbly to the other end of the

table for her things. Paige and the rest of the students silently walked away.

Anna could not remember a day as black as the day she tried to tell Paige off. Somehow, she dragged herself through the rest of her classes. Then she walked home without waiting for Randy, certain that Randy wasn't speaking to her. That evening, neither Randy nor Jessie phoned. Anna called Gooz four times, and each time his mother answered and said that he couldn't come to the phone and would have to get back to her. When he hadn't called by eleven o'clock, Anna knew he wasn't going to call. At 11:05, she tried him one more time. The Drumfields' line was busy. Purely to torture herself, Anna then dialed the Reades'. Their line was busy, too.

"You die, Beaulac," Anna whispered. "You die." Paige had started the whole mess with her lies, and Anna wasn't finished paying her back.

She sat at her desk with a blank sheet of paper in front of her. Paige hadn't suffered nearly enough, she thought. There was no way to get her to apologize—to anybody for anything. And no way to undo the damage that had been done that day. But Anna could torture Paige a little. All it would take was some imagination.

Anna sat in thought for a while. She doodled on the page. She practiced Paige's penmanship. At long last, she set a clean sheet of paper on the desk and wrote:

> Cheryl—
> Guess what? Kirk Norris likes you! He

wants to go out with you, but he's too shy
to tell you. He asked me what to do, and I
suggested a double date—Kirk and you,
Harry and me. Meet me at my house tomorrow night (Saturday) at 8:00. Wear
something nice. And *don't mention this to
Kirk*. You'll embarrass him.

                              —Paige Beaulac
P.S. I live at 27 Stone Mill Way.

Anna didn't have to make the story any more complete or believable than that. She knew Cheryl would fall
for it unquestioningly. That was how desperate Cheryl
was.

Chapter Fourteen

Finding the note from Paige Beaulac in her locker was the most exciting thing, and the happiest thing, that had ever happened to Cheryl Sutphin. It was right there on Friday morning, sticking out of the little air vent. Cheryl had read it through three times, then had tucked it in her English notebook and hugged the wonderful secret to herself all day.

Twice, Cheryl tried to talk to Paige. She wanted to ask her what to wear, but Paige seemed to be in a hurry all day. Both times that Cheryl approached, Paige ran off. Since the Sutphins had no phone, it was either talk to Paige in school or try to get to the pay phone sometime Friday night or Saturday. But at last Cheryl told herself that she was a big girl; she didn't need Paige's advice. No siree. She could figure out what to wear all by herself. And she knew where Paige lived, so that was no problem. Stone Mill Way was out where all those big houses were.

But how would she get there? Bud was going to be hauling again that weekend, so there was no one to drive her. Well, Cheryl had an old bicycle. If she could just find an outfit that she wouldn't spoil too much by riding a bike, she'd be all set.

Bud Sutphin spent Friday night out, which was fine with Cheryl. On most Fridays, Bud took himself over to McNamara's Bar and blew a good portion of his earnings on beer and chasers. On other Fridays—"Bad Fridays" were how Cheryl thought of them—he sulked at home because he didn't have enough money to join his drinking pals. Cheryl preferred the loss of their money to Bud's shouting and abuse.

Cheryl woke up Saturday morning feeling fine all over—the second time in less than a week, which was a miracle. She waited until Bud left for his hauling trip to West Virginia later that morning before she began to get ready for her date. The double date with Paige was Cheryl's very first date ever. According to the magazines she read in the library, it should be one of the most special nights of her life. For Cheryl, it would be a private wonderfulness.

As soon as Bud was gone, Cheryl began to dress. She knew exactly what to put on. The beautiful pink prom gown was really the only choice, bike or no bike. Not only was it the sole dressy dress in the Veronica box, but it made Cheryl feel more connected to her mother than ever.

"It's like being with you again, Ma," Cheryl said as she stood in front of the broken mirror in the bathroom. "If I'd known it was this easy, I'd have looked in that box long ago. It just goes to show, it's what you always said: 'You'd be surprised what you can do when you stop being afraid.' Well, I'm not afraid so much anymore, Ma. And tonight I'm going out on my first date. Even if I do have to get there on my bike I hope you'll come along."

It wasn't easy, but Cheryl biked all the way out to Stone Mill Way. When she reached the Beaulac mansion, she was surprised to see that hardly any lights were on.

Cheryl told herself not to worry. She parked her bike near the front door. Then she smoothed down her lovely dress and patted her hair. Good. All the bobby pins were in place. Only a few wisps of hair had escaped on the ride over. It was probably just as well that she hadn't washed her hair in a while.

She rang the doorbell. Then she waited so long that she almost rang it again.

Suddenly the door was flung open.

There was Paige. She looked as beautiful as ever.

She looked a little surprised, too.

Paige blinked.

Cheryl put on a big smile. "Hi, it's me," she said. "I'm here."

"Yeah?"

"I mean, I got your note. Is he here already? Kirk?"

"What?" snapped Paige.

Cheryl shuffled her feet nervously. "Is Kirk here? I came right at eight o'clock, like you said. I'm not late." At least she didn't think she was. She didn't have a watch, though.

"Like I said?" Paige repeated.

"You know, in your note."

Paige frowned. She looked slightly disgusted.

"Can I come in?" asked Cheryl timidly.

"No!" exclaimed Paige. "You can't come in."

"But . . . but . . ." Lower lip trembling, Cheryl tried to collect her thoughts. She got control over her wobbly voice. And she remembered what her mother would have said at a time like this: *Stop being afraid*.

("Stay near me, Ma," begged Cheryl silently.)

Cheryl drew in her breath. "Look here, Paige," she began. "I—I know you're the richest girl in town and I'm just about the poorest, but that doesn't give you any right to be rude to me." Cheryl bit her lip. This wasn't how her first date was supposed to start off.

"Excuse me," said Paige coldly, "but *I* am not the one standing on *your* front porch interrupting *your* evening. I don't know what you're doing here, but why don't you just go on home and leave me alone." Paige started to shut the door.

No, thought Cheryl. ("Help me, Ma.") What had gone wrong?

Cheryl stuck her foot against the door so that Paige couldn't close it all the way.

Paige began to look both frightened and angry. "Go away, pig!" she yelled. "Take your fat self and *go away!*"

Cheryl gasped, but her mother wouldn't let her give up so easily. "You said . . . you said Kirk Norris likes me. Now—"

"I said Kirk Norris *likes* you?" Paige gave a snort of contemptuous laughter. "Oh, you mean that joke in the slam book? Get real. What are you—a psycho?"

"No—no." Cheryl backed up a few steps.

Paige could have closed the door then, but instead she opened it wide and stepped outside.

"Kirk would have to be deaf and blind to like you," she said, leaning into Cheryl's face.

Cheryl was startled to find that Paige had liquor breath, just as Bud often did.

"Look at you," Paige went on. "You're dressed like some prom queen from 1952, you're fat, your hair's an oil slick, and you *smell*, Cheryl. Have you ever heard of deodorant? It's a wonderful invention."

Cheryl continued to back away. She stumbled down the steps, managed to find her bicycle, and heaved herself unsteadily onto it.

Paige was still shouting at her.

As Cheryl teetered into the darkness, she shouted over her shoulder, "I hate you, Paige Beaulac! You'll be sorry!"

All the way home, she thought, "Oh, Ma. Oh, Ma. It's happened again, and I can't take it anymore. So I'm coming. I'm really coming. Then we can be together for always."

Chapter Fifteen

Cheryl was not a planner, but she planned things *very* carefully that night. Her mind was working fast, fast, fast. By the time she was parking her bicycle at the front door to her house, she knew what she was going to do and how she would do it.

It probably wouldn't even take very long.

First she slipped off her mother's prom gown. She put it back in the Veronica box just the way she had found it the first time. Then she wiped away her makeup and took the bobby pins out of her hair.

Next to the back stoop she found a large cardboard carton. She brought it inside. She thought it would be nice to give her father a head start, so she labeled the box "Cheryl," filled it with her things, and placed it next to the Veronica box. Then she laboriously wrote a note to Bud and taped it to the side of the Cheryl box.

That done, Cheryl went into the bathroom and drew a tub of warm water. While she waited for the tub to fill, she stripped, folded her underwear neatly, and put it in her dresser drawer.

It was amazing how easy everything was. It just showed that Cheryl was no dummy. Not too many other kids at CHS could do what she was doing as well as she was doing it.

When the tub was full, Cheryl looked through the medicine cabinet. Bud didn't shave often, but he did shave occasionally. Cheryl found a brand-new pack of razor blades. She was pretty sure one was all she'd need, but she took two anyway. She didn't want to have to get out of the tub once she'd gotten in.

Cheryl rested the razor blades on the edge of the tub. Then she climbed in. The warm water was to draw the blood out. And the cutting had to be done a certain way. Long vertical lines right along the veins, not short ones across her wrists. The blood flowed out faster that way. Oh, Cheryl knew what she was doing all right. She'd read about it in a book once. Ha, ha. What would that author think if he (she?) knew how Cheryl was using those bits of information?

Cheryl tried to relax.

"Okay, Ma. Here I come. It won't be long now," she said. "The waiting is almost over."

Cheryl picked up a razor blade and poised it above her wrist.

Chapter Sixteen

"Cheryl Sutphin is dead."

Anna heard the news first thing at school Monday morning. It was all anyone could talk about, even the students in the upper classes who hadn't really known Cheryl.

Anna glanced at Randy aghast. "Excuse me?" she said to the student they had just passed in the hallway. "What did you say?"

"Cheryl Sutphin is dead," the girl repeated. "Did you know her? She killed herself. Her father found her yesterday afternoon."

"Oh, my God." Anna's head began to whirl.

"Anna? You okay?" asked Randy. Anna had apologized to Jessie and Randy over the weekend, and the girls had managed to pick up their friendship. Gooz was a different story.

"I just need to sit down," said Anna. "I'm a little dizzy. I—I didn't eat breakfast this morning."

Randy led Anna to a windowsill and forced her to put her head between her knees and take deep breaths.

What had happened over the weekend? Anna wondered. Had Cheryl gone to Paige's? She had to find out.

By the time she was sitting in her first-period class, waiting for the teacher, Anna felt better. The room was buzzing with talk of Cheryl. Anna leaned over to the student across the aisle from her, a boy she knew slightly named Garrett Meyer. "Did she leave a note or anything?" she asked, pretending that her morbid curiosity had run away with her.

Garrett was eager to talk. "She sure did," he replied. "I heard it was quite a note, too. I'm on her bus route. Everyone was talking about her on the way to school this morning."

Anna leaned over farther, as if to say, "I'm all ears."

"The note said," Garrett continued, "something about her life being gray and everybody hating her. But this is the weirdest part. You know how her mother's dead?"

Anna nodded.

"Well, she said she wanted to be with her mother again. She was going to join her or something."

That really was weird. Maybe Cheryl was just plain crazy, thought Anna. Maybe her death had nothing to do with the slam book or Saturday night.

Anna sat back in her chair and heaved a sigh of relief. That, however, was before the funeral.

There is nothing drearier than a funeral in the rain. Anna hadn't been to many funerals (just one other), but she found Cheryl's utterly depressing. She couldn't figure out if it was because she felt so guilty or because it was, in fact, just utterly depressing.

The funeral was held in a small church on the outskirts of Calvin. Anna wondered if Cheryl had belonged to the church or if it was simply convenient for Cheryl's father to make arrangements there. She realized how little she knew about Cheryl. For years, rumors about the Sutphins had flown—Cheryl was retarded, Cheryl's father was a criminal, Cheryl's mother was in the loony bin, the Sutphins only took one bath a year. What was the truth? What had Cheryl's life really been like? Anna would never know. All she had seen was a quiet, fat, pimply-faced, slow-moving girl in shabby clothes who had shuffled her way, day after day, year after year, through the Calvin public schools with a classful of students who made fun of her.

Cheryl's funeral was held on Tuesday morning at eleven o'clock. CHS students had been given permission to go to it. Ordinarily, an invitation to escape classes for a couple of hours would have met with an enthusiastic exodus from school, but Anna didn't know anyone else who planned to attend. She rode silently to the church with Cheryl's homeroom teacher.

Apart from Anna and the teacher, only a handful of
mourners arrived. One of them was Mr. Roscoe from
CHS, looking uncomfortable. Two more were middle-
aged women Anna did not recognize, a third was a
middle-aged man she also did not recognize. Then there
was the man whom the people of Calvin knew simply as Bud.

But he was a different Bud than the scruffy one Anna
had occasionally seen shoving his way out of McNamara's Bar. That Bud was often drunk and always
dressed in the same clothes—the Bud Sutphin uniform,
Anna's brother-in-law once called it. Without fail, he
had worn a plaid shirt (flannel in cool weather, cotton in
warm weather, the cuffs usually fraying), the dirtiest,
greasiest pair of blue jeans imaginable, and heavy work
boots. In very cold weather, he would add a plaid hunt-
ing jacket and cap to the uniform.

The Bud in the chapel was clean, shaven, and wearing
a suit and polished shoes. His face bore a look of an-
guish and disbelief that shamed Anna. She had always
thought Bud had been cruel to Cheryl. But what did she
know? Did the man sitting ten pews in front of her miss
his scapegoat and housekeeper? Or was he mourning the
death of his daughter? Was it possible to be cruel to
someone and love that person at the same time?

The minister began to speak, and the mourners sat up
straighter, turning their attention to him, or at least pretending to. Anna never listened to sermons or speeches,
and she didn't listen to the minister that day either. She
let her mind wander and was thoroughly startled several

minutes later by the sound of a sob tearing itself from someone's throat. Who was crying? A *teacher?*

Anna turned around with great curiosity. Then she drew in her breath sharply. Paige Beaulac was sitting alone at the end of a pew, hunched over, her shoulders heaving.

Anna felt dizzy. What was Paige doing at the funeral? She'd had more contempt for Cheryl than any other student. There was no reason for her to be there ... unless she felt guilty.

Anna slumped down. She tried to concentrate on the minister's words, but it was hopeless. Outside, the rain beat on the roof of the church. Soggy leaves slapped against the windows. In front of her, Bud put his head in his hands and wept. Anna shivered.

Paige began to cry harder, and Anna was tempted to go to her. But she couldn't make herself. After a while, Paige's sobs lessened.

For the millionth time since Anna had first heard the news about Cheryl, she wondered what had happened on Saturday night. Cheryl must have gone to the Beaulacs'. She had probably talked to Paige. How much had she said? Had she brought the note with her? What had Paige said? Anna had no answers.

Finally the service was over. The people filed outside for the burial. Going to the burial was the very last thing Anna wanted to do, but she had no choice. The teachers were staying. It was miles from the church to school.

Both Anna and Paige hovered at the back of the little crowd gathered under the plastic awning in the cemetery.

Anna was surprised to realize that while Paige seemed grief-stricken, she herself was feeling nothing but vague fear.

She stood still, watching as the coffin was lowered into the grave, as Bud, still weeping, limply tossed a handful of earth onto it, and as the minister said a few more words. Wasn't there some old saying about a sinner having to be buried outside the walls of a church graveyard? And wasn't it a sin to take your own life? Not that Anna wanted to see Cheryl given a sinner's grave. It was just something to think about.

At long, long last, the people turned and began to leave. The minister put his arm across Bud's shoulders, but none of the others, not even the CHS teachers, so much as looked at each other.

Anna found herself standing next to Mr. Roscoe and asked him for a ride back to school.

"Was Cheryl a friend of yours?" Mr. Roscoe wanted to know as they pulled away from the church.

"No," replied Anna. "She didn't have any friends."

"None?"

"Not one."

"And you . . .?" Mr. Roscoe's unasked question hung between them. *What were you doing at the funeral, then?* he wanted to know.

"I—I don't know. I just felt I should be there."

Mr. Roscoe nodded. "Not one friend," he repeated to himself, as if he couldn't believe it.

Chapter Seventeen

Halfway back to school after the funeral, Anna suddenly realized that she was going to throw up—soon. She told Mr. Roscoe she didn't feel well and asked him if he could please drive her home instead of back to school.

Mr. Roscoe's parting words as Anna dashed into her house were, "Feel better, Anna. It's hard when friends die."

Friends. Mr. Roscoe just couldn't believe that Cheryl truly didn't have any . . . had never had any.

Anna ran inside and did throw up. Twice. Mrs. Wallace pronounced her a victim of the stomach flu and sent her to bed. Anna knew better but was glad for the privacy of her room.

She crawled under the covers with the slam book in her hands.

It was lunchtime. In the CHS cafeteria, the students would be clamoring for the slam book.

Anna heaved a sigh and leaned back against her pillow. Was she the popular one, or was it the slam book? How popular would she be without the slam book? The book was a crutch, a prop. Without it, Anna might fall over.

Owning the slam book was kind of like being rich or having famous parents. You never knew whether kids liked you because of your money or parents—or because you were you.

Now was Anna's chance to find out, and she was afraid.

And yet . . . Cheryl's body was, at that moment, being buried beneath the earth of the Church of the Covenant cemetery. The soil was clumping down and the rain was chilling it, and Cheryl's body would be cold and unforgiving.

Another wave of nausea swept over Anna.

Cheryl was dead, and Paige needed a straitjacket, and Anna and Gooz weren't speaking, and none of it would have happened if it weren't for the slam book. Anna stared at its mottled cover. Most of the white blotches had been filled in. They were red or green or blue. The binding on the side was coming off. The edges of some of the pages were soft from being thumbed through. The book looked old and warm and friendly. It was well disguised.

Anna threw back the covers. She carried the slam book to her closet and hid it in an empty box. She put the box under a stack of *Seventeen* magazines and covered the magazines with a quilt.

It didn't seem safe enough.

She unburied the book and looked around her room.

Nothing seemed safe enough. Anna wanted the book out of sight and away from any place her mother might find it, but not quite gone. She couldn't bring herself to be completely unconnected to it. The slam book was a parasite, yet Anna felt sure she'd be dead without it.

At last, she pulled a row of books away from their shelf, slid the slam book behind them, and shoved the books back.

There. The slam book was gone (sort of). No one would find it. But Anna hadn't cut herself loose from it.

Chapter Eighteen

Anna returned to school the next day. For the first time since ninth grade had begun, she didn't take the slam book with her. She checked its hiding place twice before she left the house, afraid it would be found, afraid it would disappear.

At school, the kids easily accepted Anna's excuse that she had forgotten the book. Most of them were busy talking about Cheryl anyway—speculating, wondering. Not a single Sutphin joke circulated.

Anna felt numb and disassociated from her friends, although she sat at her usual table.

Randy, uncharacteristically somber, accompanied Anna home that afternoon. They sat in Anna's room and listened to tapes, not talking. When the phone rang,

Anna reached for it as if she were in a slow-motion dream.

"Hello?" she said. "What?" She motioned for Randy to turn off the tape deck.

"Who is it?" Randy whispered loudly.

"Jessie," Anna replied quickly, holding the receiver away from her mouth. "She sounds hysterical. I can barely understand her."

"Do you want me to talk to her?" asked Randy.

Anna shook her head. She listened, anguished, for several more seconds. "Jess— Jess—" she said, trying to break into her friend's unintelligible torrent of words. At last there was a second of silence on the other end of the phone. "Jessie," said Anna, "I can't understand you. Talk more slowly. What's wrong?"

"Nothing!" came the excited reply. "Mom's back! Can you believe it?"

"Your mother's *back?*" cried Anna. "Oh, Jessie, that's wonderful!" Anna cupped her hand over the receiver and whispered to Randy, "Her mother's back!"

"So I hear," said Randy, smiling.

"I have to go!" said Jessie. "I have to talk to her!" Jessie hung up the phone with a clunk.

Anna hung up, too. "Wow," she said. "I really didn't think this was going to happen."

"Me neither," said Randy. "If I were Mrs. Smith, *I* wouldn't go back."

"I wonder what happened," mused Anna.

"I'm sure we'll find out soon enough." Randy's gaze traveled around the room and lit on Anna's bulletin board, where a wallet-sized school photo of Gooz was tacked up.

"Hey, Anna?" said Randy.

"Yeah?"

"What's going on with you and Gooz? Anything?"

Anna shook her head. "We haven't spoken since . . . that day. But you know how he hasn't been sitting with us at lunch?"

"Yeah?"

"Well, it's not like he's *really* mad. I mean, he's not going out of his way to avoid me. He and Tim sit just one table over. And he hasn't changed any of his routes to and from classes, even though we see each other in the halls a lot. I wonder if he would talk to me if I called him now. That first night, he was definitely avoiding me, but I haven't tried calling him since then. And we *do* have to finish our project."

"Do you want me to leave?" asked Randy.

"Oh, no. I didn't mean that. If I call him, I'll do it in the evening."

"You know, I think Gooz is really pretty down to earth," said Randy. "He doesn't seem like the type who'd play games."

"No," agreed Anna. "He isn't. And he had a right to blow up on Thursday. I wasn't being fair to anyone that day. Not even to Paige, really, although I can't forgive her for the things she did."

"There's something about the slam book," Randy began. She paused.

"I know," said Anna uncomfortably. "I put it away. I

never thought it could get so..." *(Deadly?)* "... I mean, Peggy—my cousin Peggy?—her slam book had some jibes at kids, some comments about being overweight and stuff, but ours... well, it started with Paige's comments, and everyone went overboard."

"Maybe you didn't read Peggy's closely enough," suggested Randy quietly. "Maybe there was more in it than you saw."

"Maybe," said Anna miserably.

"Where is the slam book, anyway?"

"Hidden."

"Where?"

"Just hidden. Don't worry. I won't bring it to school. If other people want to start one, let them. Let everything be on *their* heads instead." Anna could feel tears starting.

"Hey," said Randy. "What's wrong? And what do you mean, 'be on their heads'?"

Anna hesitated. It would be so easy to get the slam book and show the whole mess to Randy. At times, Anna felt she would burst if she didn't tell.

But she was too afraid.

The moment passed.

The phone rang again. Anna reached for it. "Hello?" She paused, listening. "Jess—

Randy frowned at her questioningly.

"Jess—" Anna tried again. Then, after a pause: "Come over here. Are you listening? Come over here right now. Okay?...I'll see you in a few minutes, then." Anna hung up the phone. "Oh, God," she said, dropping her head. "Oh, God. I don't believe it. Jessie's mother only came back to get the rest of her things. I didn't understand much of what Jessie said, except that her mother has left again, and this time Jessie thinks it's for good. She'll probably want to stay here for a while. I better alert Mom."

Anna ran downstairs, followed by Randy. She found her mother in the den, paying bills.

"Mom," said Anna. "Jessie just called. Twice. She thought her mother had come back. I mean, she *had* come back, but only to leave again. Jessie's on her way over, and she's really upset. Can she stay with us again? If she wants to?"

"Of course," said Mrs. Wallace. She put the checkbook away and went into the kitchen. "Let's be ready with some tea. We'll try to talk calmly and find out exactly what's going on."

Randy pulled Anna aside. "Do you want me to stay or to leave?" she whispered.

"Oh, stay, stay," replied Anna. "Jessie would want you here. You know that—don't you?"

"Just checking." Randy laughed uncomfortably.

Anna put her arm around Randy. "You and Jessie and I," she said. "We're the Three Musketeers. We've got to stick together."

"Right," agreed Randy with a smile. "One for all and all for one, or however it goes."

The doorbell rang.

Anna and Randy looked at each other. "Steel yourself," said Anna.

Mrs. Wallace followed the girls into the hall, and Anna opened the door.

Jessie was standing on the stoop with a duffel bag full of clothes and her schoolbooks. Her hair was a mess, her clothes were rumpled, and her eyes were puffy and red.

"Here she is," said Anna shakily. "Miss America."

No one laughed.

Jessie stepped inside, and Mrs. Wallace embraced her. "Come on in the kitchen, sweetie," she said after a moment. "We've got tea ready."

"Tea and sympathy," Anna added, and this time a smile played around Jessie's lips.

Four gloomy people sat at the Wallaces' kitchen table for over an hour that afternoon. Jessie poured out her story. Then they talked and planned and wondered.

"When I got home after school," said Jessie, "Mom was sitting in the kitchen drinking a cup of coffee. I was so thrilled I didn't know what to do. I hugged her, then I called you, then Mom and I started to talk. And she said she was sorry I thought she'd come back, that she hadn't meant to raise my hopes. She said she was just there to get the rest of her things and that she wanted to leave before my father came home.

"She told me she got a good job in New York and she's going to move there. She's already found an apartment." Jessie paused. "I don't understand why she didn't tell me any of this before. I mean, she could have prepared me for it.

"The thing is," she went on, "I don't really feel abandoned. Mom said I can come live with her. She said she'll let me know when she's settled, and then I'm free to go to New York. She wants me there."

"That's great!" exclaimed Randy at the same time that Anna exclaimed, "New York! But that's so far away!"

Mrs. Wallace looked thoughtful. "What do you want to do, honey?" she asked Jessie.

Jessie shook her head. "I don't want to stay here with my father and Jack, and I don't want to move to New York. That's for sure."

"Why not?" asked Randy. "We'd miss you like crazy, but wouldn't you like to live in a big city?"

"Not at *all*," said Jessie. "Not for one second. Think of what goes on there. Crime and murder and rape and drugs."

"But what *do* you want to do?" asked Mrs. Wallace again.

"I want Jack and my father to go to New York and Mom to come here and live with me."

The others laughed.

"Realistically," amended Anna's mother. "What do you want realistically?"

"Realistically, I haven't the vaguest idea." Jessie's voice shook. Anna could see her eyes glistening.

Then Jessie shoved her teacup aside, put her head in her arms, and began to sob.

Anna and Randy looked at her helplessly.

When at last Jessie sat up and dried her eyes, Mrs. Wallace asked, "Does your father know about this yet?"

Jessie shook her head miserably.

"Did your mother leave him a note or anything?"

"A letter," Jessie replied. "Very official. The envelope is typed, and the return address is a lawyer's office in New York."

"I guess we should wait until your father sees that before we ask if you can stay with us for a while. Don't worry, Jess. Mr. Wallace and I will talk to your father this evening. We'll convince him that you need a little time with us."

"Thanks," said Jessie, and wiped her eyes on a napkin.

Anna looked at her friend, who'd just had the rug pulled out from under her. She thought of Cheryl and Paige.

She felt as if her safe world were falling apart.

Chapter Nineteen

When Mr. Smith heard that Jessie had escaped to the Wallaces', he marched right over. Anna's father had called him soon after the Wallaces were through with supper. Mr. Smith had just finished reading the letter from the lawyer. "I'll be right there," he said stiffly.

"Anna! Jessie!" Mr. Wallace called upstairs. "Can you come down here for a moment, please?"

The girls abandoned their homework.

"What is it?" asked Anna as they reached the living room.

"Jessie, your father's on his way over."

"Oh, *no*," groaned Jessie.

"It's all right," said Mr. Wallace. "We'll talk to him. I just wanted you to know what's going on."

Mr. Smith showed up several minutes later.

"Jessie," he said as soon as he stepped inside, "do you know anything about this?" He waved the letter at her.

"Well, I don't—"

"Excuse me," interrupted Anna's mother. "Why don't we sit down? Greg, would you like a cup of coffee?" She ushered everyone into the living room.

When the coffee had been poured, Anna and her parents and Jessie and her father sat looking uncomfortably at each other.

Jessie was the first to speak. "I saw Mom," she told her father. "I don't know what the letter says, but I can guess. She's gone for good, Dad. She's moving to New York."

Mr. Smith nodded briefly.

"Jessie's pretty upset," said Anna's father. "We'd like her to stay with us for a while, if that's all right with you."

"What, again?" said Mr. Smith. "What's the matter, Jessica? Our house isn't good enough for you?"

"Well, you're hardly ever home, Dad," said Jessie. "And—and I miss Mom."

"I don't see how imposing on the Wallaces is going to help anything."

"Oh, she's not imposing, Greg. You know that," said Mrs. Wallace. "We love to have her here. Anna needs a friend around, too. She's practically an only child."

"All right," said Mr. Smith wearily. "All right."

"Thanks, Dad." Jessie jumped up and kissed her father on the cheek. Then she and Anna ran upstairs before he could change his mind. But they heard the sounds of

the adults talking for a long time, their voices rising and
falling.

"Jess," said Anna later that night as they were ready
to turn out the light. "I'm really glad you're here."

The following evening, Anna called Gooz. It was
eight-thirty. Jessie was doing her homework in the
kitchen. Anna's parents had gone to a movie.

Gooz answered the phone himself, obviously not expecting to hear from her.

"Hi, Gooz," said Anna in a small voice. "It's me,
Anna."

There was silence on Gooz's end of the phone.

"Gooz?"

"Yeah, I'm here."

"I think we need to talk."

"I guess you're right."

"I've put the slam book away, Gooz. It's hidden. I
won't bring it to school again."

"Why didn't you *throw* it away?" asked Gooz accus-
ingly.

"I—I don't know," Anna replied. "But it won't be
back in school. I promise."

"Anna, I want you to know"—Gooz paused to take a
breath—"that I'm not mad at you. I just felt we needed
some time apart to think things over."

"Okay," said Anna, "but I just want *you* to know that
everything I said about Paige was true. She did all those
things. She even caused the problems between you and
Casey."

"Well, not really. Like I told you, we were already having problems. The slam book just started the fight that brought them out in the open."

"Then why were you so upset with me?"

"Why? For two reasons," answered Gooz, "which I thought were plain to see. First of all, the Anna Wallace I saw shouting in the cafeteria that day was not the Anna Wallace I knew. You said some pretty rotten things."

"Paige *did* some pretty rotten things," Anna interrupted.

"And you put your friends on the spot, especially Randy, and you embarrassed me. How do you think it looked for everyone to see that you, of all people, knew that Paige made up that comment in order to break Casey and me up?"

"Not great," Anna mumbled.

"My friends were saying that you *let* Paige write that just so we could start going out."

"That's not true!" cried Anna. "Paige was the one who wanted to go out with you."

"I'm just telling you what they were saying," said Gooz.

"I'm sorry."

"Then, of course, I had to apologize to Casey, which was the last thing I wanted to do," Gooz went on.

"You talked to her?" asked Anna carefully, hoping to hear more.

"Yes. I had to. Thanks to you, Casey and I and the whole world all found out what happened. I couldn't just let it go by. I had to talk to her."

"What did she say?"

"Not much. But I think she was glad I apologized."

"Gooz, I really am sorry about the scene in the cafeteria. I didn't want it to get so out of hand. I just wanted to teach Paige a lesson. She's been doing horrible things."

"Maybe it's not your place to teach people lessons," Gooz said quietly.

"Paige used to be my friend," Anna replied. "As a friend, I thought I owed it to her to—"

"Humiliate her? Embarrass your other friends?"

"Okay, okay, I handled it badly. I already said I was sorry."

"I know you did. I'm sorry, too. I guess I'm over-reacting because of all the flak I've been getting about us."

"Maybe we could try to start over again," suggested Anna cautiously. "After all, we have a project to finish."

"Do you want to sneak off campus and have lunch at the diner tomorrow?" Gooz asked. Anna could almost hear him smiling.

"I'd *love* to," she said.

"Great. I'll meet you at your locker at the beginning of lunch period."

"Okay! I'll see you then!"

When Anna hung up the phone, she found that her hands were shaking. But she ignored them and ran to the top of the stairs. "Hey, Jessie! Come here!" she cried. "Excellent news!"

*　*　*

Anna dashed to her locker the next day as soon as she could escape from her classroom. She stuck her books inside and pulled her jacket out. Then she waited for Gooz, all the while afraid that he wouldn't show up.

But he did.

He was holding a daisy in front of him, and he offered it to Anna. "I stole it," he confided. "From the horticulture lab."

Anna stuck it through a buttonhole on her coat, Gooz took her elbow, and they walked down the hall and out of school.

Petrinferno's Diner wasn't far from CHS, and soon Anna and Gooz were seated in a booth near the back. They ordered their lunches without looking at the menu. Then they sat in uncomfortable silence.

"I have this crazy urge to blow my straw paper at you," said Anna, just to break the silence.

"I'll blow mine if you'll blow yours," replied Gooz.

Anna giggled. They they shot their papers at each other.

"Boy, is it ever good to be eating lunch with you again," said Anna. "I've really missed you these last few days."

"Me, too," said Gooz. "I was upset at first, but I still missed you."

Anna nodded.

"You looked so awful on the day we heard about Cheryl," Gooz went on. "The day of her funeral, too. I wanted to say something to you, but I couldn't."

"That whole thing took me sort of, um, by surprise," said Anna. "It was scary."

"Very," agreed Gooz. "My father was telling me how many kids commit suicide each year. It's practically an epidemic."

Anna didn't know whether to feel better or worse. So Cheryl was just one of thousands. But would she have killed herself if Anna hadn't sent her to Paige's?

Suddenly Anna felt tears in her eyes.

Gooz noticed immediately. "Hey, what's wrong?" he asked.

Anna shook her head and dabbed at her eyes with a napkin.

"Cheryl?" asked Gooz, frowning.

Once again, Anna was tempted to pour out the whole messy story. But she didn't dare. "No," she lied. "I'm just so happy to be sitting here with you."

Gooz smiled. "I honestly didn't know I meant so much to you. No offense, Anna, but sometimes you're hard to figure out."

"Well, I missed you."

The waitress brought their hamburgers. Anna found that she had lost her appetite, but she managed to force down about half of her meal.

Gooz looked at her questioningly. "I don't think I have a very good effect on you," he said.

"It's not you," Anna told him. "Really."

Her happy mood had been broken. Anna found that she could think of no one but Cheryl.

Chapter Twenty

"Oh my God! You got it already!" exclaimed Anna.

"I don't believe it!" said Jessie. "When did you get it? *How* did you get it?"

Randy grinned. "Just this afternoon," she replied. "And I only had to wait on line an hour."

"An hour. That's not too bad," said Jessie.

It was a Friday afternoon. Anna and Jessie had been summoned to the Taylors' house moments earlier by a gleeful call from Randy. Their favorite group, PT and the Uptown Boys, had just issued a five-record album. It came in a handsome box, was expensive, and was very much in demand. Anna had heard of people waiting in lines for six hours or lining up at a store before it had opened, even before the sun had risen. And now here was Randy with the real thing, and on a Friday afternoon, too. A weekend of music stretched ahead of them.

"If you don't mind my saying so," Anna said, "this isn't really like you, Randy. I mean, I'm *thrilled* that you got the album, but . . ."

"I make exceptions for PT," Randy replied, shrugging.

"Well, let's look at it," said Jessie excitedly.

The girls sat on the floor and bent over the album. Randy had somehow managed to wait until her friends came over before she lifted the cover. She raised it— and the phone rang.

"Darn," said Randy. "I better answer it. Tanya's not here, and Mama's in the middle of something downstairs."

"No, I'll get it," said Anna. "Randy, you go ahead and open the box. You deserve to. But don't play anything without me!"

"Thanks, Anna," said Randy.

Anna dashed into the hall and picked up the phone. "Hello, Taylors' residence," she said.

"Ish Anna there?" asked a slurred voice.

"Anna? This is Anna . . . Paige, is that you?" Anna could barely hear above the sounds of Jessie and Randy gasping and squealing over the album.

"Ish—ish Anna there?" The voice sounded confused.

"Paige?" Anna said again, an uncomfortable feeling in her stomach. "What's going on?" Anna turned toward Randy's room. "Hey, you guys," she whispered. "Come here."

Jessie and Randy got to their feet and stood in the

doorway to Randy's room, leaning against the doorjamb and looking curiously at Anna.

"Hello?" said Anna. "Paige?"

"Anna? Ish that—that you?"

"Yeah."

"Boy, are you hard to track down . . . hard to . . . hard to find. I called your housh"—Paige paused—"and Jeshica'sh housh. Who'sh housh ish thish? Randy'sh?"

"That's right," said Anna. "Listen, are you okay? You sound funny."

"Funny!" Paige cried. She started to laugh, but it was a low, moaning laugh, completely unlike her, although it did remind Anna of something . . . or someone.

Anna racked her brain. Mrs. Beaulac. That's who Paige sounded like. "Paige?" said Anna. "Are you drunk?"

There was a long pause. "Huh?" asked Paige sleepily.

"Have you been drinking?" Anna asked again.

"Coursh," Paige managed to say.

"Why—why are you calling me?" Anna stammered. She put her hand over the mouthpiece and said nervously, "Paige has been drinking. I don't know what's going on."

"I want," Paige said, ". . . want to tell you about the . . . the crocktail I made. I mean, the cocktail. . . . It was a V and V . . . vodka . . . and Valium."

"Valium!" screeched Anna. "How much?"

"My God," said Randy softly.

"Oh, about . . . about half a . . ."

"Half a what?"

"Half a . . . bottle."

Again Anna put her hand over the receiver. "She drank vodka and took half a bottle of Valium!"

"Find out where she is," said Randy.

"Paige, where are you?" asked Anna, trying to sound calm. "Are you at home?"

"Shnug ash a rug in a bug . . . bug in a rug . . ."

"*Are you at home?*" Anna repeated more slowly.

"Home ish where the . . . where you . . ."

Anna turned to Randy and Jessie again. "I think she's at home, but she's not really saying."

"Ask her once more," suggested Jessie.

"Paige," Anna tried again, "where *are* you?"

"Where am I?" Paige repeated. "I don't know. Don't even know who I am." The slurred voice was becoming softer and more difficult to understand.

"Look around. What do you see?" asked Anna.

"I shee . . . white. And booksh. Shoft rug."

"Are you in your bedroom?"

There was a long silence.

"Paige? Are you in your bedroom?"

Clunk.

"Paige? Paige?" shrieked Anna. "*Paige!*"

"What? What?" cried Jessie.

"There was this thud," said Anna, "and then nothing. But she didn't hang up. The connection's not broken. I think she dropped the receiver or something."

Randy grabbed the phone from Anna. "*Paige!*" she yelled. "*Paige!*"

"What in heaven's name is going on up here?"

The girls turned to see Mrs. Taylor standing at the top of the stairs.

"Mama!" Randy cried. "Paige called. She's still sort of on the phone. She sounded awful, and she said she drank some vodka and took half a bottle of Valium. I think she passed out or something."

Randy's mother took the phone. "Paige?" she said urgently.

No answer.

Mrs. Taylor hung up. "Do you know where she is?" she asked the girls.

"We're pretty sure she's at home," replied Randy. "But we're not certain."

"All right. You call the paramedics and tell them to go to the Beaulacs' immediately. I'm going to run next door and ask Mrs. Gregory to watch for Tanya. Then I'll take you to Paige's."

"Okay," said Randy. "Okay."

Mrs. Taylor dashed downstairs. Anna and Jessie put their coats on while Randy made the call.

"What did they say?" asked Jessie as they were piling into the car.

Mrs. Taylor pulled into the street, tires squealing.

"They're probably already on the way," replied Randy. "The guy who answered said they'd go out immediately."

"Is Savanna there today?" asked Mrs. Taylor.

"She should be," replied Randy.

"Good. She can let the paramedics in if Mrs. Beaulac isn't home. I probably should have called Savanna before we left."

"Well, we got the paramedics out there, anyway," said Anna. "That's the important thing."

The rest of the mad drive was spent in silence. When Mrs. Taylor turned into the circular drive in front of the Beaulac mansion, the girls saw that the paramedics were already there. The ambulance was parked in front of the house, and a stretcher was being lifted into it. Savanna stood just outside the door, wringing her hands.

Mrs. Taylor drew to a stop and everyone piled out.

"Savanna!" called Randy. "Paige phoned us. That's how we knew."

"I can't believe it," exclaimed Savanna. "She came home from school this afternoon in a wonderful mood. I had no idea what she was doing."

"What did the paramedics say?" asked Mrs. Taylor.

Savanna shook her head. "They're not sure."

"Where's Mrs. Beaulac?"

"In California. Palm Springs."

"Why don't you try to reach her?" suggested Mrs. Taylor. "The girls and I will go to the hospital to be with Paige."

Anna, Jessie, and Randy clambered back into the car, and Mrs. Taylor sped to the Calvin Medical Center, the sound of the ambulance siren preceding them all the way.

The ambulance pulled into a side entrance and up to a parking area marked *Emergency Parking: Authorized*

Vehicles Only. Mrs. Taylor had to park elsewhere. By the time they'd found the visitor's lot, gotten their receipt, and dashed back to the emergency room, Paige was nowhere in sight.

"Was Paige Beaulac brought in?" Mrs. Taylor asked the woman behind the desk in the waiting area. "A young girl? The ambulance just brought her."

"Oh, the overdose," said the woman crisply.

Anna sank into the nearest chair. "Oh, God. Oh, God."

"Where is she, please?" Randy's mother asked.

The woman nodded to the treatment cubicles beyond a set of swinging doors. "She's being worked on."

"How many of us can be with her at once?"

"Oh, I'm afraid you can't go back there," replied the woman. "Not while they're treating her."

"Well, is she going to be all right?"

"They won't know for a while. Listen, do you know how I can reach her family?"

"Her mother's her only family in Calvin, but she's in California right now. The housekeeper is trying to reach her."

The woman nodded. "Maybe you can answer some questions for me."

"Of course," replied Mrs. Taylor, "but just a moment, please." She turned to the girls, who were sitting stiffly in a row of chairs that were not only hooked together but bolted to the floor.

"How is she?" cried Anna, jumping to her feet.

"They're not sure yet." Mrs. Taylor put her arm

across Anna's shoulders and guided her back into her seat. "They're working on her now. We won't be able to see her for a while. I'm going to phone Savanna and then try to answer a few questions for the nurse. Why don't you get yourselves some sodas or something from the machine over there?"

The girls didn't feel like sodas. They sat in tense silence. After a moment, Anna called her mother to tell her what was happening. Jessie tried to reach her father but wasn't able to.

Randy's mother phoned Savanna, then spoke to the nurse.

Savanna and Dwight showed up and also talked to the nurse, then to Mrs. Taylor.

After what seemed like forever, a young doctor came through the swinging doors. The nurse pointed him to Mrs. Taylor, Savanna, and Dwight. He approached them grimly. They conferred for several moments before Savanna followed him back through the doors.

Anna, Jessie, and Randy got to their feet. "Mama?" asked Randy.

"The doctor said she's stable," Mrs. Taylor told them. "She's not out of the woods yet, but they've done all they can do for the time being, and they're moving her to a room. Savanna spoke to Mrs. Beaulac, and she's going to get the next plane back here."

Anna hadn't heard most of what Randy's mother had said. "She's not out of the woods yet?" she repeated. "Oh, God, this is all my fault. It's all my fault." Anna began to sob loudly.

Randy looked at her curiously. "All *your* fault?"

"That's what I said, dammit." Anna's voice was rising. "It's my fault, it's all my fault, it's my fault, it's all my fault!"

"Anna," said Mrs. Taylor sharply. She sat her down.

Jessie sat next to Anna. She leaned over, put her head on her arms, and began to cry, too. "I can't take this," she wailed. "I really can't."

Chapter Twenty-one

It seemed like the longest night Anna could remember. Her parents picked her up and brought her home from the hospital, dropping Jessie off along the way. Then they took Anna to her room, told her to lie down, gave her a cup of tea, and asked what was going on.

"It really *is* my fault," she told them miserably.

"What is?" asked Mrs. Wallace. "I don't understand."

"Paige tried to kill herself because of something I did." Anna started to cry again.

"Honey, I don't think—" her father began.

"Dad, *listen* to me." Anna couldn't keep the story a secret any longer. She hated to burst her parents' bubble about their daughter, but it had to be done. She retrieved the slam book and held it out to them. "It started with this," she said tearfully. "It's called a slam book. Peggy had one," she went on as her parents turned the pages. "She said how popular it had made her, and how cool it was to start one. And it was so *hard* being a freshman at CHS—I mean, really awful—and I guess I wanted to feel important again. So I started this slam book.

"It was great at first. Jessie and Randy and Paige and I were the center of attention. Everyone got to know us right away. We always had a big crowd of kids to sit with at lunch."

"So far," said Mrs. Wallace, "this doesn't seem too bad. Some of the comments aren't very nice, but... what happened?"

"People started using it the wrong way," Anna replied. "They started writing things in it just to hurt other people's feelings. You know, kids they were mad at or something." She turned to Casey Reade's page and pointed to an entry near the top. "Paige Beaulac wrote that, but it's completely untrue. She made it up because she wanted Casey to break up with Gooz Drumfield."

"Your Gooz," Mr. Wallace said thoughtfully.

"Yes. And it worked. Only Paige had wanted Gooz for herself."

"And that didn't work," said Mrs. Wallace.

Anna shook her head. "Gooz doesn't like Paige. He started going out with me."

"Did you know then what Paige had done?" asked Anna's father.

"Yes," replied Anna. "I was there when she wrote it. Jessie and Randy were, too. I didn't know what to do, though. Anyway, Paige was furious with me for ending up with Gooz. And she was mad at Randy and Jessie. Just for being my friends, I guess. I don't really know. Actually, she was mad at everybody. She started writing terrible things in the slam book." Anna pointed several of them out to her parents.

"Why, that's horrible!" Mrs. Wallace exclaimed when she read the Oreo comment. "Poor Randy."

Mr. Wallace turned to Anna, puzzled. "I don't see that you've done much of anything wrong," he said. "Paige seems to be the one who's caused all the trouble."

"Well, the thing is," said Anna, "it got to the point where I wanted to get back at Paige. I wanted to do something to embarrass her, to make her look bad or silly, the way she was making the rest of us look."

Anna's parents glanced at each other.

"So . . . you know Cheryl Sutphin?" Anna went on.

The Wallaces nodded grimly.

"Well, she has a page in the book. Everyone was writing really rotten things about her. So I wrote a couple of nice comments on her page—but in Paige's handwriting." Anna showed them Cheryl's section. "Everyone saw the notes. Paige must have seen them, too. No one really knew what was going on. They all thought it was just some sort of practical joke, either on Paige or on Cheryl. No one found out I wrote them. Anyway, Cheryl didn't think they were a joke. So of course, she started acting like Paige's best friend. Paige was so embarrassed she didn't know what to do.

"I might have let it go at that, except that Paige and I had a huge fight—right in the cafeteria—and thanks to some things that came up, Randy and Jessie got mad at me, and Gooz and I sort of broke up for a while. So," said Anna, drawing in a deep, shaky breath, "I sent a note to Cheryl from Paige telling Cheryl to go to the Beaulacs' for a double date with Paige and these two guys. It was just supposed to be a joke on Paige."

"But it was a cruel one," said Mr. Wallace. "It was especially cruel to Cheryl. You *used* her, Anna."

"I know, I know." Anna's voice trembled.

"And?" prompted her mother.

"And Cheryl went. I'm sure of it. I don't know what happened, but it was later that night that she killed herself." Mrs. Wallace gasped. "And then Paige turned up at the funeral. I think she was feeling guilty about something.

"So you see? It's all my fault. I killed Cheryl and I almost killed Paige."

Anna dissolved into tears again, but quite unexpectedly her mother took her firmly by the shoulders and shook her once to get her attention. "I want you to understand something, young lady," she said. "What you did was wrong. It was unforgivable. But you did *not* kill Cheryl, and you did *not* force Paige to swallow vodka and Valium this afternoon. Both of those girls were very troubled to begin with, or they wouldn't have reacted the way they did. Do you really think if you had pulled the dating trick on Randy, for instance, that she would have slit her wrists?"

"*No,*" replied Anna, taken aback.

"That's because Randy is a well-adjusted young

woman. She has her share of problems, but she handles
them in a healthy way."

"And," added Anna's father, "I don't believe that
Paige actually intended to kill herself. What she did
seems more like a cry for help. If she had *really* wanted
to commit suicide, she wouldn't have phoned to tell you
what she was doing. She called you in time to save her
life."

"Yes," said Anna slowly, wiping her eyes. "I guess
so."

Mr. and Mrs. Wallace left Anna alone for a while.
When they returned, they had obviously discussed the
situation.

"As soon as Paige is well enough," said Mr. Wallace,
"you're going to talk with her—in person—and tell her
what you did, show her the slam book."

"Oh, *Dad*."

"You are then," Mrs. Wallace continued, "going to get
rid of the slam book, and I don't mean hide it. I mean
throw it away. And after *that*, you are to have nothing to
do with slam books. Not one of your own, not Peggy's,
nobody's."

"That's no problem," said Anna. "I hope I never lay
eyes on another one in my whole life."

"We'd like you to talk to a counselor, too," Mr. Wallace said. "I think you need to straighten a few things
out."

"See a *shrink?*" cried Anna.

"It depends on how you look at it," her mother replied. "I just think you need to talk to an unbiased adult."

"Well . . ." said Anna. "Maybe I do. Okay. I'll talk to someone if I have to. I'll try anything—once."

"Oh, Lord," said Mrs. Wallace. "I hope not."

Anna smiled. Then she opened her arms, and her parents crowded in for a hug.

When they left a few moments later, Anna suddenly felt as if she couldn't stand to be alone with herself. She got up and wandered around her room. She gazed blankly out the window. When she heard the phone ring, she made a dash for the extension in her parents' room. She didn't care who was on the other end of the line. All she wanted was a distraction. But it would be nice to hear from Gooz.

"Hello?" she said.

"Hi," replied Jessie's subdued voice.

"Oh, Jess," said Anna, and the whole horrible hospital incident came flooding back to her.

"I'm sorry I—I'm sorry about what happened this afternoon," said Anna. "I mean everything—crying, making a scene, you know."

"I'm sorry too," said Jessie. "But Anna, I really understand—"

Tears welled up in Anna's eyes and threatened to spill over. "Don't you dare say anything nice to me!" she exclaimed. "I'll cry all over again."

"Then listen, I'll tell you what's been going on."

"Going on?"

"Dad and I have been talking. And I mean *really* talking. Me talking and Dad listening, and Dad talking and me listening. Not just yelling at each other and not listening at all. And guess what? Dad's going to call that drug hotline number and talk to somebody about Jack."

Anna was amazed. "How on earth did you convince him to do that?"

"I told him that in a way Jack was committing suicide just like Paige tried to do, only he's doing it more slowly. It's the same thing, as far as I can see. Just as self-destructive. And I told him about Cheryl. A suicide and an attempted suicide. It really got to him. He *finally* listened. I think he's worried about me, too."

"I can't believe you actually said that," said Anna.

"Me neither. But Paige really scared me today. It could have been Jack on that stretcher." Jessie paused. "We talked about Mom, too. And, Anna, she isn't coming home. I didn't know this, but Mom and Dad have been in touch. By phone, I guess. Dad knows more than I do. He seems resigned and kind of sad. He says it's too late to patch things up. Mom's in New York for good, and they're working on the divorce papers."

"Oh, Jessie. I'm sorry."

"Well, now *I'm* going to cry."

"I'll stop being kind," Anna teased.

"No, it's not that. I think I'm going to move to New York. I'm going to visit Mom over Thanksgiving and see how I like it. And if I do move there, I'm just going to miss you . . . so . . . much. . . ." Jessie's voice broke as she burst into tears.

Then Anna was crying again, too. She didn't know whether to be happy or miserable. She felt as if all the people she cared about were slipping away from her and she was powerless to stop them.

Chapter Twenty-two

The hospital smelled funny. It smelled of medicine and detergent and bland food and rubbing alcohol and sickness. And it was too brightly lit. Anna hated it. But she was able to admit to herself that what she really hated was what she had to do. Hospitals were no picnic, but confronting Paige would have been unpleasant anywhere.

Paige was in Room 214, a private room, of course. No roommate or ward for her.

Anna approached the door slowly. It was ajar. She peered through the crack, but all she could see was a wall.

She knocked.

No answer.

She knocked again.

Nothing.

"Paige?" Anna called softly. She pushed the door open and peered around it.

Paige was curled up in bed, her back to Anna.

Anna thought she was asleep until she saw her foot move.

"Paige?" Anna tiptoed into the room and around to the other side of the bed. She wondered where Mrs. Beaulac was.

"Oh, boy. Just the person I wanted to see," said Paige sarcastically.

"Gosh, look at all your flowers," said Anna, gazing at the windowsill and tables.

"Don't be too impressed," replied Paige. "They're all from Mother. When I'd been here for two days and the only flowers to arrive were from you and Jessie and Randy—even my father didn't send any—she decided it was disgraceful and arranged for the florist to deliver me a fresh bouquet every morning."

"Oh." Anna remembered the bag in her hand and gave it to Paige. "Here," she said. "I don't know if you're allowed to have this, but I thought you might be tired of hospital food."

Paige looked in the bag and a faint smile played on her lips. "White chocolate," she whispered. "You remembered."

"How could I forget?" said Anna, grinning. "First thing you ever shoplifted. Only this is bought and paid for."

Paige closed the bag. Her smile disappeared. Anna

noticed the dark circles, almost like bruises, that shadowed her eyes. Her skin was sallow and waxy.

"So . . . how are you doing?" asked Anna. Then she laughed self-consciously. "Dumb question, huh?"

Paige shrugged.

"But really. How *are* you doing? I mean, when do you get out of here?"

Paige shrugged again. "Don't know. Whenever they decide I'm not suicidal anymore. I have to see a shrink."

"Yeah," said Anna. "Me, too."

Paige finally looked interested. "You? How come?"

Anna could feel herself flushing. "Paige, there's something I have to tell you."

"What?" asked Paige suspiciously.

"Can I sit down somewhere?"

"Sure. Take all the stuff off that chair. You can just dump it on the floor."

Anna did so and drew the chair up to the bed.

Paige sat up.

"I want you to read something." The slam book was waiting in Anna's purse. She withdrew it and handed it to Paige.

"The slam book!" Paige exclaimed. "I do not want to read that. Why do you want me to read it? Hasn't it done enough damage already?" She sounded slightly hysterical.

"There's only one page I want you to see." Anna turned to Cheryl's page.

"Cheryl?" said Paige, her voice rising.

"Shh. Just read the last few comments."

With a sidelong glance at Anna, Paige took the book. "Yeah? So what? Someone copied my handwriting."

"I did," said Anna.

"You?"

"It was just a joke," Anna said quickly. "Just a joke. You were being so horrible, and I wanted to get back at you, so I fixed it so Cheryl would start hanging around and embarrassing you. Really, I only thought it was funny.

"But then I—after I wrote the stuff in the slam book, I sent her a note from you telling her to go to your house that night for a double date—Cheryl and Kirk, and you and a boyfriend I made up for you. I guess it worked," Anna said lamely.

Paige sat up. Her sallow complexion was reddening. "You bet it worked! She showed up. But I didn't know why. I said horrible things to her. I yelled at her, and then she *killed* herself!"

"Keep your voice down," said Anna nervously. "Someone'll come in or something."

"All this time I was blaming myself, and it's *your* fault!" Paige went on.

Anna bristled. "I may have sent her over there, but I wasn't the one who yelled at her! You did that."

"Girls, girls. Please." A disapproving nurse stuck her head in the room. "What's going on in here?"

"Nothing," said Paige sullenly. "We're sorry. We'll quiet down."

The nurse left.

Anna and Paige stared angrily at each other.

"Look," Anna said finally, "I came over here to tell you what happened. I wanted you to know about Cheryl, and I don't think either of us is to blame. I shouldn't have played the joke on her, and you shouldn't have yelled at her, but we didn't kill her. I've played jokes on plenty of people who haven't committed suicide, and I bet you've yelled at plenty of people who haven't committed suicide."

Paige managed a small smile.

"Well," said Anna, "I better go. I just wanted you to know the truth."

"That's what slam books are for, right?" said Paige.

"Right," said Anna. "You'll never see the slam book again, though. My parents are making me throw it away. By tomorrow, it'll be out at the dump."

"Where it belongs," said Paige.

Anna stood up and put the chair back where it had been.

"'Bye, Paige," she said as she slipped out the door.

"'Bye," Paige replied. "And thanks."

Anna turned and left. It was to be the last time she and Paige would see each other for two years.

Chapter Twenty-three

Two months later:

"So this is New York, huh?" asked Jessie. She and her mother were standing on the observation deck at the top of the Empire State Building. Jessie had been in New York for four weeks, but this was the first time she had seen the city from a height, spreading in front of her in all directions, a tangle of buildings and streets.

"This is New York," agreed her mother.

"I must be crazy," said Jessie.

"Why?"

"To want to live here."

"I don't think you're crazy," replied Mrs. Smith.

"You always were prejudiced where I'm concerned."

Mrs. Smith put her arm around her daughter. "I have a right to be. I hope you know how happy I am that you made this decision."

Jessie smiled. "It wasn't an easy one. Especially with Dad and Jack finally starting to get things straightened out."

"Maybe Jack will want to visit New York sometime."

"He could come when I go back to Calvin for vacations. Sort of an exchange program."

Jessie's mother laughed. "Well, come on, roomie. We better go. Our apartment awaits. There are dirty dishes in the sink, and baking to be done."

"And homework," added Jessie. "I still can't get over that A in English. First one I ever got."

"I knew you could do it, given the right environment."

"Yeah, pollution, noise, traffic . . ."

Arm in arm, Jessie and her mother headed for the elevator.

Paige stood on the steps to the front door of her home. Earlier that morning she'd walked through the house and all around the property. She had taken a long last look at everything. Now she was impatient to leave. Her suitcases and trunk sat beside her. Whenever Dwight brought the car around, he could load her things in and she'd be off.

It was typical that her mother was away and only Savanna was there to say goodbye. But Paige didn't really mind. She and her mother had said goodbye two days earlier, and Mrs. Beaulac had seemed honestly sorry that she'd be in San Francisco when her daughter left for England.

Furthermore, for once Paige was looking forward to starting over. A boarding school in England would be *really* different. Mrs. Beaulac had been lucky to find a school that would accept Paige, but she'd done it, and Paige was happy to be leaving Calvin behind. She felt stronger than she could ever remember and had a good feeling about England. The only thing she regretted was not saying goodbye to Anna and Randy, or writing to Jessie. But Paige had been out of school ever since that awful day, and she just couldn't face them. Maybe she'd write to them from her new school.

Dwight brought the silver Cadillac to a stop in front of the house. He stepped out, opened the trunk, and began packing the suitcases in it. Savanna poked her head out the front door.

"Come say goodbye to me inside, honey," she said. "It's freezing out here."

Paige ducked inside, Savanna held out her arms, and Paige rushed to her.

"I'm really going to miss you, Savanna," she said. "And I won't see you for ages. Probably not until next Christmas if Mother really intends to spend the summer with me in Europe."

"Well, we'll make it one fine Christmas, then," said Savanna. She released Paige.

Paige looked searchingly into her eyes, then turned and fled outside. Dwight had just finished putting the trunk in the car.

"Thanks, Dwight," said Paige. She buckled herself into the front seat, and Dwight slid behind the wheel.

As they drove away, Paige stared down at her hands. She didn't want to think about what she was leaving behind, only about what lay ahead.

Randy never admitted to anybody except her mother that she was relieved her little clique had been broken up.

"It was getting scary," she told Mrs. Taylor. "It was intense. And I felt trapped with them. Anna and Jessie are still my friends, but I think what happened was for the best."

"How's Anna doing?" asked Mrs. Taylor.

"It's harder on her than it is on me. She misses being the center of attention. Without her clique, she's not Miss Popularity anymore. But she and Gooz are still going out, and somehow she just seems . . . calmer. She started writing for the newspaper, and she said she's going to try out for the basketball team."

Randy paused and looked sadly at her mother. "But you know what I feel like sometimes?" she asked.

"What?"

"I feel like a shell on the beach. A common shell that no one notices. And a wave comes along and washes over me, then recedes, and I'm still right there on the beach, no one noticing me."

"Oh, honey," said Mrs. Taylor. "If other people could put that feeling into those beautiful words, they'd do it. Because every adult remembers feeling that way. And every teenager *does* feel that way. It's part of being fourteen or fifteen or sixteen and trying to become your own person. I guarantee it'll change."

"You *guarantee* it?"

"I do."

Randy grinned. "Good. What a relief."

The phone rang, and Randy jumped a mile. "I'll get it!" she screeched.

"Expecting a call?" asked Mrs. Taylor.

"Yeah," replied Randy. "There's this new boy in school. . . ."

Ring, ring.

"Hello?"

"Hello, Anna?"

"Yeah?"

"It's your sister, stupid!"

Anna giggled. "Sorry. I was expecting—"

"Gooz?"

"Well, yes."

"Listen, I'm sorry I'm not Gooz, but I've got something to tell you."

"What?"

"You're an aunt again."

"Aughh! I don't believe it! Where are you? In the hospital? You mean you already had the baby?"

"Yup. She came a little early."

"*She?* Oh, excellent! It's a girl. I can't believe it! Seth's got a sister! How are you? Is the baby okay? When did you have her?"

Hilary laughed. "I'm fine, Tom's fine, the baby's fine, and I had her at one o'clock this morning. She weighed six pounds, six ounces."

"Ooh, she's little."

"But perfectly healthy."

"What did you name her? You wouldn't tell us the names you'd picked out."

"That's because if the baby was a girl, we wanted to surprise you."

"Surprise me with what?"

"Her name is Anna. Anna Wallace Rogers."

"Oh Hilary. . . . Thank you. I don't know what to say."

"Nothing, sweetie. Just promise you'll come visit your namesake soon, and put Mom and Dad on the phone, okay?"

"Okay—and I promise!"

Anna called her parents to the phone and then wandered into her room. She sat on the bed, thinking. Her namesake. She'd teach the little Anna all sorts of things. She'd teach her how to cross the street safely and not to talk to strangers. She'd teach her how to bake chocolate-chip cookies and how to hit a baseball. And she'd tell her stories about Hilary before Hilary became a mother. She'd read all her favorite childhood books to her, too. But she'd tell her that no matter what, she should never open a slam book, because it was like Pandora's box. The big Anna would tell the little Anna to stick to *Winnie-the-Pooh* and *Charlotte's Web* and *Doctor Dolittle*. They were much, *much* safer.